I0760403

RED HONEY

First published 2024 by Fahrenheit Press.

ISBN: 978-1-914475-73-3

10 9 8 7 6 5 4 3 2 1

www.Fahrenheit-Press.com

F 4 E

Red Honey

Collected Short Stories

By

Saira Viola

Fahrenheit Press

Also by Saira Viola

- *Jukebox*
- *Crack, Apple & Pop*

"I'll tell you what Freedom is to me: No fear, I mean really, no fear!"

-Nina Simone

INTRODUCTION

The way it went down, one minute I'm at my desk with a newspaper and coffee, the next a short story submission comes in from Saira Viola that prompts me to sit up straight. Right from the start with a through-line to the here and now, it's a rush to enter Saira's lively, descriptive fictional world, replete with trenchant social commentary that reminds me of one or two literary greats I won't name, if only to err on the side of understatement.

Hey—I'm just a guy who reads for pleasure. But when it's time for a book, you'll find me in the most comfortable chair in the house with something good in my hands.

From what I can tell, the Muses, Athena, the whole pantheon of applicable goddesses get in on the action when Saira sits down to write. That is, if you notice the embarrassment of uncannily vivid sentences as they go by. Though that's just part of it. You're treated to a divine arrangement of assonance and alliteration, a steady rat-tat-tat, thereby putting you in a trance. Let me suggest that Saira's international background (Africa, London, LA, New York) contributes to the effect. She draws from a diverse well of experience in concert with her sense of rhythm and vibrant imagination. I've surmised that as with the aforementioned deities, gold tracers follow in Saira's footsteps.

Since I went all in on understatement, though, I'll close with a note about social commentary. Saira's characters might be buried in debt, lacking the means to find their way out. Or they might be at the mercy of crooked cops. Syd Du Frais in "The Future's A Fraud" is a painter of dystopian works in a dystopian world. Or the London barrister Dempsey Loveitt, while perceptive and articulate enough to know what's afoot and how to describe it, is no less susceptible to the pull of the underworld.

But the one I arguably love the most is Saira's full-on prose poem about Ginger and Ichabod in "Profit and Loss (A London Story)." Both of them adrift in the hobo jungle, looking for relief. As in the works of one or two of those literary legends I could mention, the dreadful yet beautiful karmic path comes alive in the mind's eye.

What else can I tell you? Go find that comfortable chair.

Todd Robins, Editor of Vautrin Magazine,
Wichita, May 2024

CONTENTS

MONKEY FIZZ

It's wall-to-wall porn star martinis at TriBeCa Beach. The nouveau penthouse disco located on the rooftop of the Standard Hotel. A red-eyed waiter adds another table to a stack of three as jaded models, bawling socialites and diamond-toothed preppies bitch and gossip in the corner. They have mortgaged faces and continuous lucky day smiles with delicate manicured hands and cloud soft hair. Phones are strictly off limits. This glam palace is simply too exclusive for snappy snaps and selfies. A little after ten o'clock: Kat Sloane aka Anne Tucker, petty drug dealer, sex worker, grifter and law school dropout with a growing sadistic streak, shimmied through the lobby in inky chiffon as the floor pulsed with the remixed scat of Cardi B's *Money Bag*. "La la la," she cheeped like an irritating parrot. Her flip of blond hair twisted into a chic voguish top knot as she pranced into view. Sleek. Standing at 5'5" in stylish flatties, she surveyed the scene like an iron-bellied big cat on safari. Her mind lost in a pistol of crime. She tossed her head and bounced up to a table, beaming at a slew of demi-celebs and rich snobby Manhattanites. Behind the faux veneers, and twinkly torches of polished laughter the pouty shouty princess kitties were ready to claw each other's eyes out for the star seducer of the night: William Balfour the III, owner of the priciest real estate on the East Coast and last male heir to a global drug empire. Unlike his big monied name Balfour was a puny little fuck with an everlasting shemozzled look on his rich, entitled face. His thin red aquiline snout constantly in other people's business making deals, buying, selling, arranging takeovers, and licensing everything from condoms to cigars. Raiding companies and running them into the ground was his favoured MO. Balfour had a candida infection in his mouth, spoke with a pronounced daffy-duck lisp, and wore nylon briefs to bed, but all the ladies lurved him.

Roz Sedgwick, a swan necked brunette, wrapped in white taffeta, invited Kat to sit beside her. "Dahling you look gaw jus. Mwah."

An exchange of air kisses. Kat slunk back on a cushy blue velvet armchair. "He should have been here eons ago."

Roz yawned. "Dahling he's probably in a meeting with his mother. She's the one who runs the show."

Kat and Roz were part of an ugly universe where souls were kicked around, sold, rented, and pawned for short term highs. And everybody who was anybody was tripping off molly rolling off LSD or snow-blowing their way to the Hamptons. She gave Roz a knowing glance. "You ready?"

"Yass!"

She took out a couple of Barbie pills, handed one to Roz and slipped the other in her mouth.

Kat was in a bitchy mood but ready to rhumba. She slapped the table and started singing the first lines of ÇA *Plane Pour Moi* by Plastic Bertrand. That insanely catchy French pop song now forever immortalised in a Rice Krispies ad. When she got to the high notes and the oooh-wee-oohs, Roz stuck her tongue out and joined in.

They toasted the night with another round of Stolli.

Stinky Colitas

Secretly, Kat was up to her neck in debt. She had borrowed heavily to fit in with this exclusive coterie of pretty young things. Capped teeth. Butt and Boob jobs. Anus bleaches. Cheek implants and lasered pubes had forced her to sell a little bit of herself every week in credit instalments. Now she was under extreme pressure to repay the crippling 175 percent interest on the loan she'd taken. Nobody knew that Kat hadn't eaten for three days. Like a hungry spider spinning a web for a juicy black fly, she waited… She only had one week left to pay off Milky Kong, king of the underground banking system and proprietor of Speedy Cash Finance. Milky didn't do barbecues, Sunday church services or excuses. He drank his long island iced tea from a special bone china cup and thought Tuesdays were unlucky.

Kat had a fucked-up plan: Bamboozle Balfour into a charity swizz with a story about a fake heiress and get Milky off her back. *Or maybe I'll just …slash his smug little face. Killa clown style and take what I need from the safe.* She'd have to do everything herself of course. She couldn't rely on anyone. Anyway, she had no family except crabby aunt Wilma who'd reported her to the cops twice for participating in a Ponzi scheme.

The last time Kat felt like she had a real friend was when she was six years old. The endless conveyor belt of goading toadies she now had to outsmart over and over again, weren't friends, they were greed–infected golden birds, endowed with healthy plumage and a protective halo of family money.Her face crawled with tension. A funnel of hives, ready to erupt across her brow.

"What's wrong sweetie?" Roz asked. Not remotely interested.

Kat squinched her eyes into a frown. What she wanted to say was: I got an eviction notice from the landlord and a final demand from the electric company, I've missed two car payments, and I've been living off top shelf ramen for months. I can't afford to get my wisdom tooth pulled or even buy a jumbo pack of tampons plus I'm using fish mox from Petco as an antibiotic. But she just shrugged and said, "Money stuff."

Roz stared dumbly at the sequin of posh noshes around her. Like so many privileged fuckwits blessed with generational wealth and the might of daddy's plastic, she found it extremely hard to talk about money. Harder than having sex with strangers or doing bumps of cocaine with schizophrenic poets in public bathrooms. She quickly switched topic. "Dontcha just lurve Hayley's dress? Soooo cute. It's super fantastic. Did you hear about Courtney and Evelyn?"

A blank look.

"Courtney and Evelyn were you know, and Pete caught them at it in Courtney's pool house…"Roz paused for dramatic effect. "Pete wanted to put the whole thing on Tik Tok so Courtney..."

All Kat could hear was blah blah blah. And *pool house.* She eyed a glass of single malt on the table opposite and wanted to smash it with her fist.

Kat couldn't even ask Roz for help. It was like an impenetrable wall. A wall of dollars that divided them, cemented by human blood. Kat was starving, but Roz had no idea or simply chose to ignore it.

Kat found hanging out with the super-rich exhausting. There were all these unspoken rules she had to navigate, and Roz made it quite clear that talking about money was considered extremely impolite in her sunny circle. She thought of the ugly rent demand sitting on her dresser and sighed. Captioned in blood red letters, it was like a loaded gun just waiting to go off. She found it taped to her door when she got home one night. It was official. She'd been named and shamed. She remembered reading about The Great Plague in history class. They used to mark the doors of plague victims with a big red cross. Now centuries later they slapped eviction notices on debtor's doors, letting the whole world see their misery. Kat bit her lip. *Debticide sounds like a fucking contagious disease.*

Just then Balfour limped into view. He was speed talking on his cell phone. A spaced-out shaggy haired busser rolled his eyes. Balfour knew no one would dare tell him to put the phone away. Rules didn't apply to people like him. "I don't give a fuck if she's six months pregnant she owes me money. Either she pays up in full by noon tomorrow or I'll fucking smoke the bitch out if I have to. I'm not running a goddam homeless shelter here." Red-faced, he ended the call and surreptitiously slipped the phone back into his pocket.

Roz waved him over with a huge smile. "Dahling. You look super fantastic…"

Kat wanted to vomit all over Roz's pristine white dress. *She doesn't care I'm fucking hungry because people like her have already eaten and I'm still greasing the floor looking for crumbs.*

A nondescript bellyache got up so Balfour could sit down, as a waiter whizzed over and trotted out the usual spiel. Balfour ordered a whiskey and let his credit card do the rest of the talking.

Three booze-bombed hours later, away from all the other nameless flowers in the Presidential Suite at the Standard hotel, Kat hung around like a limbless pup waiting for the right moment to strike. Propped up on a smattering of bar snacks and vodka, she had numbed those hunger pangs but couldn't shake the bad feeling that swirled around in her glottis and squatted on the cleft of her chest.

Roz, oblivious, sat in creamy, isolated splendour trying to drink away the night. Balfour played with the fly of his pants.

Kat watched them both with jealous eyes… *Freedom. They have pure freedom…* I *could never buy that kind of freedom I'd have to marry it steal it or…*

Balfour opened the safe and foolishly announced the access code to everyone in earshot, using an overly hammy James Bond accent: "Left 00 Right 71 and open sesame weeee!"

Roz and Balfour giggled like two greasy piglets. They were in their own protective bubble. Roz nudged him when they saw Kat hovering next to them. Balfour looked down his nose at her and whistled. "When did all that sweet sugar turn to shit?"

Kat thought *fuck you* and a fury of dark thoughts ran riot in her head like a train of silver fish.

Roz popped her eyes wide. "Dahling tell Wills about Tiffany Van Day. She's setting up a nouvelle charity auction. For people just like us. Rich famous super-switched on, socially woke and you know changing the narrative, you have to join… you have to change the narrative."

Kat was about to say something when Roz dismissed her with a flick of her wrist. "Be a sweetie and chop up some more blow."

She whipped off a dinky hollowed out love heart from her neck and handed it to her with a matching spoon. Her expression said it all. Kat was still an outsider, and that narrative would never change. Kat slouched off to the bathroom and in a harsh sing-song voice muttered, "Not your fucking maid bitch. Sick of wet nursing these Manhattan blue bloods." Then she pulled out a pack of razor blades from her purse and cut the tip of her ring finger just for fun. A spangle of blood needled her hand as she thought about shanking Balfour in the eye.

In a grumpy gangster hangout on the West Side, Milky Kong was holding court with a rag tag of nodding bulldogs. Milky got his nickname because he was built like a mammoth gorilla, and drank at least two pints of milk every day. A greedy smile started at the corner of his lips and ended on his second chin. His hair arranged in silver waves was parted at the side and matched his carefully trimmed salt-and-pepper stubble. Dressed in a dandyish ensemble with English leather shoes, he was surrounded by the bad, the beautiful, and the buzzed-up.

A small, virile looking oddball with wiry rimmed specs and a harsh bullying voice pigeon-stepped towards him. He checked his hairline in the wall mirror and patted down several stray greys. "Two more years that's what I got left in this business. Two more max."

A naked light shot out from the backroom and the slippery little man crawled into view. He nodded at Milky and joined him at his table. Diana Ross lulled the smoochers onto the dance floor, straight into Loveland. But Milky was in battle mode. He had dirt to shovel. "Eddy. You look exactly the same. Peanut-faced asshole."

"Thanks."

"This is personal. This is business. Always an unpleasant mix but you gotta do what's necessary."

"Understood."

A tense pause. Eddy had a tinny voice. "You know, when I got your message, I was surprised. You and Rockie been through it all…"

Milky motioned Eddy to be quiet and his face tightened. Vengeance spoke through the folds of his skin. "Everybody's got a set of rules a code of honour. You gimme me your word. And in our business, that's all we got. That's what stops us from becoming filthy, fucked up pigs."

Milky was a stickler for tradition and liked to romanticise his vocation in the same way other people waxed sweet on TV shows.

"I still got questions."

"Shoot."

"Would he really be crazy enough to double-cross you?"

Milky laughed silently. "Don't insult me. I know what I'm doing. We can sit here fucking around, pretending that things are okay. But we all know when a member of your own family tears open your chest squeezes your balls and steals your money. You gotta do what's necessary."

He picked away at a pink scab in his ear. "You know what savaging is?"

A blank look.

"It's when a female pig gives birth then kills and eats her new-born babies. A pig like that needs to be euthanised. Shot. Electrocuted. Or slowly, anaesthetised. It's just a matter of economics. Inevitable in swine production."

Milky's heavy-lidded eyes screamed BETRAYAL.

"Everybody knows if you got big plans, a big mouth, and a plane ticket to Rio, the chances of you ending up with a little lead in your skull are pretty fucking good."

Eddy raised his thick bushy brows and wormed around in his seat.

Milky took a dainty sip of his long island ice tea. "I've lost track of all the buy-ins and buy-outs. Everybody makes money out of us. The cops, the judges, the parole officers, the lawyers, the media, even those churchy jihadis with their fucking moral crusades. Now the ultimate kick in the balls. I gotta deal with insiders trying to SCREW me over."

He reeled forward and threw up. As if his stomach couldn't take any more lies.

Green vomit landed all over Eddy's hands. Eddy sprang back but it was too late. Milky wheeled forward, pulled out his semi-automatic hellcat and shot him three times in the head. A collective gasp from a hushed crowd. They watched Milky calmly mop his shirt sleeves with a napkin as Eddy lay face down in a pool of blood. Milky got up, peeled off a roll of C-notes from his pocket and flung them onto the table. He shook his head as he marched out.

"Sometimes you get chicken. Other times you get feathers."

Aftermath

Kat was hard at work. Rouge et noir were the colours of the night. Buttoned up in borrowed executive silk. She sat opposite Balfour in his private bedroom. They had been partying non-stop for forty-eight hours. Roz had passed out in a glittery mess on a swanky chaise longue in the main suite when Balfour got the itch to play kinky sex games.

Kat spied an opportunity and did what was asked. Balfour wore a two-piece Brooks Brothers suit with a peachy pink negligee underneath, black suspenders and a pair of red satin undies. Kat put on a starchy undertaker's voice and pretended to be a shrink. "So how long have you been having these uh fantasies."

"I've always been turned on by women's lingerie. I like thaaa feel of it between my fingers and thhhh way it drapes across my balls. It feels better than sex, better than money…"

Kat followed the routine, and listened to him jowl about how big and hard he was. Then after an hour or so, Balfour handed her a thousand bucks. It was an easy-peasy way to score cash. Kat thought of all the heiresses and sports stars and precious rich people who would pay to keep those kind of secrets buried. A sex scandal like that, despite the new anything-goes sexual terrain, could easily be leaked to the press for a tidy sum and sweep away all of her debt at the same time.

Of course, Balfour's family reputation would be destroyed for good, but she'd be free as a bird. She let the thought swim around in the entrails of her mind but balked at the idea of becoming some common snitch; a nasty little bottom feeder sharing snippets of sleaze to the tabloids. Instead, she ran her tongue across her lips and whispered, "Wanna try something… a little more exotic?"

Balfour's eyes lit up like two dancing mayflies. "Sure."

She slunk off the bed and shuttered the blinds. Then she peeled off her own purple panties, crawled back onto the bed and jammed them inside Balfour's mouth. He nodded at the bed stand and put his hands forward, literally begging to be tied up. She rooted around inside the drawer and spied a smorgasbord of whips, candles, some sketchy looking electrical gear, and a beautifully crafted small hunting knife. She grabbed an extension cable and bound his left arm to the bedpost, doubling down with thick duct tape.

Looking at him lying there, she was reminded of a suckling pig on a silver tray with an apple in its mouth. She moved in close and stared at the satellite of red spots that stalked his brow and the sides of his cheek, then licked the back of his ear. He grunted like an overheated skunk. His groin and armpits wreaked of stale sweat mixed with Calvin Klein's obsession. A sickly combo.

As he writhed around, she cooed and petted him, then he jerked himself off with his right hand and made a weird little squeaking sound.

Kat was relieved and repulsed. She carefully took her scrunched up panties out of his mouth. He drooled a little and let out a short breathless sigh.

"Yeah. That hit the spot."

Kat nodded politely, untied Balfour, then with a burst of extreme confidence and viperish charm, trotted out some million- dollar bullshit about a Saudi princess, ending her spiel with, "I can't believe I met Her Royal Highness Reema Bin Saud at the Edison's!"

"The who?"

Kat modulated her voice down to a persuasive purr. "The Edison's. You know the sophisticates who always have a charity chug every Sunday night at The Knicks? She reminds me of a young Nicole Kidman, and he looks like a slimmer version of Alec Baldwin, you know the Edisons. They're in real estate, made all their dough in blue chip stocks."

Balfour was visibly rattled. He'd never heard of them. They must have heard of him. Why hadn't he been invited? He was a member of the Knicks. As a grade A narcissist, Balfour couldn't bear the thought of being left out of anything, as naturally he thought everything revolved around him.

Kat played on this fear and smiled to herself. "Teddy Auberlay's pledged five thousand, but I told Reema you could easily double that. I told her you're old money mixed with new blood, and you should headline the event. She's putting on a gala and the proceeds are going to orphaned monkeys. A nice safe chimpanzee charity. It's gonna be super fantastic!"

Balfour sneered. "Teddy Auberlay's a phony. Strictly small time. Nickel and dime shit. I had to get my lawyer to throw out all his tenants when I bought his building. Maybe five families. They were like fucking rats clinging to the walls. I got rid of all those parasites I…"

Then all at once out of nowhere Kat leapt off the bed, grabbed the knife from the box, then swung back and charged at Balfour as he burst into grisly, almost ecstatic laughter. His cold mocking eyes shuttled her reflexes and SNAP! BLAT! She jammed her knee into his neck and still he laughed until she plunged the knife in between his ribs and finally his laughter gave way to a cracked scream. He slumped onto his side, clutching his stomach and gurgled, "Mom mom…"

Kat stared at his bleeding belly as the red-throated night swallowed him whole. Then in a soft voice she whispered, "It was the way you said… *rats and parasites*, like they weren't even human."

Kat kept the knife, pocketed the cash out of the safe and

skipped out of the room, quietly humming fragments of the old Donna Summer classic. "She works hard for the money… so hard for it honey."

THE END

PAYDAY

Mark Schneider. Law school dropout. Part-time drunk. Serial masturbator. High-functioning meth addict. Sex bot devotee. Ex-husband, and one of LAPD's finest.

Early morning: Parked outside Baby Blues in an unmarked grey Chrysler 300, still code 3 equipped. His white shirt unbuttoned, revealing a full pecan-tinted rug. Cuff sleeves turned back. His black pants were unzipped, and his cock poked out of striped jockeys. Schneider had a sock missing and a solitary long frizzy white hair dangled from his left nostril. Checking his face in the rear-view mirror, he yanked the hair out. "Son of a bitch. You still got it." He ran the tips of his fingers down the right side of his face. A face, chequered with mistakes, money fights, and unreported murder.

Schneider smoothed his shirt down, zipped up, and rummaged around in the back seat. Sifting through paper coffee cups, potato chip packets, a half-drunk bottle of Jameson, and a dozen grease-spotted Five Guys burger bags, he grabbed his anti-perspirant stick. Twist. Click. He slicked both armpits. Then he spied a little mouthful of sunlight. A sparkly-faced cutie, Marla Cortez, skipped right in front of him. She had just finished her shift at the Golden Banana and was on her way home. Marla had to take care of her mom, who had a heart condition, and her little brother Oscar.

She flung off her denim jacket, revealing a sea green tube top, and hiked up her skirt, allowing the youthful rush of summer heat to embrace her as she wheeled her hips around.

Her pink-string tanga on show. High High High. Smilinghonkers on display. She was all taste as she hop-scotched towards the patrol car, caterwauling, tuneless karaoke style rhymes, with a Kool-Aid cup in her hand. Her apple shaped ass winking. Jiggle. Jiggle Jiggle. Like the soft round sound of a Tenor trombone.

Schneider's smutty eye preyed on Marla's intoxicating euphoria. "Fresh."

He leant back in his seat, slid his hand down to his leg, and winced as he lifted the hem of his pants. A dime-sized hole in the middle of his right calf dripped blood. He blotted it dry with a stained paper towel and tossed it in the back seat.

"Small fish are easy prey," he muttered. "Pat and frisk. Every curve. Inside thigh and sugar walls." He opened the car door using the Dutch Reach technique, so he could easily spot any on coming distractions, or potential witnesses. "Excuse me miss."

Marla was in her own kookookechoo bubble. A boho suede purse hung from her neck. "Yeeeeeh."

"Could you please step this way?"

"Er… what for?"

"Coz I asked you to."

Marla sniffed.

"You got no right to ask me anything Officer. I'm notdoing anything wrong. Lemme pass please."

Schneider looked at her like a captive animal. "You ain't shit baby. You ain't nothin' and you ain't going nowhere."

"But I've done nothing wrong."

Schneider's power was sewn up tight in the furrows of his face.

Marla tried to side-step away, but Schneider blocked her path with his leg and showed off his gun tucked in his waistband.

"Sir. Please. Just let me through."

"No. Fucking. Way."

Marla spat on the ground. "What the fuck is going on." Under her breath she hissed, "Bbbbbbastard!"

"Whooooa. Eassseee tiger." Without blinking, Schneider pinned her arms behind her back and used his left hand to control her. Within seconds, she was cuffed. He forced her to stand against the car legs apart and placed his big meaty fingers around her waist. After patting her down, he groped her left butt cheek. "You got your ID?"

Marla flinched.

Then he groped her right butt cheek.

Her eye lashes instinctively quivered "D…Don't touch me!"

"Cool it honey. You're slurring your words, and there's that crazy eye twitch. You reek of weed and pcp. And you're in

trouble. It doesn't look good for you. Not at all. No mam. Thing is liddle lady, I'm entitled to touch. Anywhere I want. Cos, I got a feelin' you're concealin.' And your freaky-deaky necked shit makes me think you're under the influence of a drug or controlled substance. But I'm a nice guy. I'm thinkin' you and me can work somethin' out." He caught the warmth of her body as he stood behind her with his cock pressed hard against her ass and slipped his fingers into the back of her panties. "You know what I want."

Marla opened her mouth as wide as she could, her tonsils trying to spread the injustice. "Arrrrrrrrrrrrggghhh!"

Schneider lunged deeper and squeezed her snatch. "One more word and I'll fuck the shit right out of you."

Marla tossed her head back and mule-kicked him in the shin.

He stumbled, picked himself up and untied the purse from her neck. "Now what we got here? Some kind o' prairie hippie shit?"

Inside her purse, Marla had her driver's license, cell phone, a tiny tube of cherry lip balm, an EBT card, and some foil wraps. Schneider held the purse under his right arm, walked her to the other side of the car, then placed her headfirst into the front passenger seat. He sat on the driver's side and pretended to run her intel through his police laptop. "We got a real messy situation. Clearly, you're under the influence of some kinda drug probably some alkhi – hol too. Completely outta control in a public place. So, you're a danger to yourself and everyone around you."

He held up the foil wraps. "And what we got here? Some leftovers? A little angel dust. Krissst."

Schneider's face grew uglier. "Girl you're fucked! Well, what's it gonna be big Jim and the twins or a trip to the precinct and county lock up? Get down girl. C'mon. Get down."

A string of tears beaded Marla's eyes. "You wa...want mmme t'suck yoooo off th… then y yyou let ...me go?"

"That's right."

"Bbbbbbastard!"

"I saw the EBT card. Dunno why they bother with that shit. You can't buy jack. No vitamins, no beer, and no cigarettes. So, what the fuck's it good for? If you accept my offer, at least you'll be getting a dose of good ol' American protein. Just you and me. It's a very generous offer."

Marla clawed her own hands. A form of self-protest. "Wh..what kind of fucked up po-po are you anyway?"

"The real kind. Dirty. Reliable. Now we got a deal or what?"

Schneider unzipped his pants.

"Now give it a long, slow suck lollipop style…"

Schneider forced her head down. One hand gripped the back of her neck. Pastel ribbons of vomit began to build in her glottis.

Schneider's 45-calibre Kimber Classic was aimed at her the whole time.

Marla felt as if her tongue was buried in white America, as if she had no control of her own body. Terror. She wanted to run. Run from his blistered thumbs and his sickly cologne. But one look at his malign little eyes and she hung on, like a trapped bird feeding her wounds into a deadly snake. When it was over, she remained perfectly still for a while, staring out of the window at a singing wave of blue sky.

Schneider dropped her off at a vacant parking lot near Family Dollar minimart. She sat on the curb and threw up. A five-minute technicolour barfing opera. All her dreams, missed opportunities, and nightmares splattered to the ground.

Schneider adjusted his pants and drove away, spanking the tarmac at speed. Pounding on the steering wheel, he screeched the lyrics to AC/DC's *Highway to Hell*: "No stop signs... no one's gonna slow me down." In the cavities of his mind, Schneider believed he was a renegade, reacting against a system he'd stopped believing in long ago. To everyone elsehe was a lyin' dealin' snortin' stealin' crooked cop. The god of the unflushed crapper feasting on fresh blood.

THREE WEEKS LATER in Brodies Food Mart, Marla watched as Schneider punched open the cash register and jammed his pockets with a stack of bills. The owner simply shrugged and turned away. Marla had been marking time: At the Rape Crisis Center in West Hollywood. At the Free clinic for contact dermatitis. At the unemployment office. At Danny G's pawn shop hocking her sick mother's wedding ring so the family could eat. They were being squeezed left and right centre for car payments, credit card bills, and back rent but all she could think of was the greying stink of a dead white fish. She followed Schneider out of the door and hovered in a side street all the while fingering her small silver Milagro she carried around for luck and her newly acquired pocket-knife. *You look like a big fat sweaty pig standing there waiting ...just waiting for the slaughter.* Schneider whistled at a petite strawberry-blonde wearing a tight lavender sweater over black jeggings and long black boots. She glanced at him nervously and hurried away. Schneider was about to say something when suddenly out of the shadows two beef heads covered by ski masks fired three shots into the air

BAM ! BAM! BAM!

They raced towards a blacked-out Lincoln pushing past a phalanx of party goers waving their hands in the air. The driver in the Lincoln spun around and caught Schneider reaching for his gun, radioing for help. The driver jammed the brakes, calmly pulled out a 38-caliber from the glove box and shot the serial masturbator straight through the window. He arched over. His legs splintered and he took the full fall on the rump of his ass. Screams! A swash of blood and a welling crowd.

"I'm hit Jesus I'm hit."

Squad cars and an ambulance arrived a few minutes later.

Marla edged her way through the rabble and stared at a sputtering red neon sign above her.

PAYDAY.

THE END

THE HALF SHELL OF SATURDAY NIGHT (Flash)

Bouncer was a multilingual trainee pastry chef and part time member of Rude Kink, a female punk ensemble. Once She stabbed a man so hard his intestines were bulging out of his belly, but she felt nothing except a perverse taste of sugar in her mouth.

Inside Klub A: A blend of suburban pastels and greying turtlenecks in block shoes were battling the dance floor. Bouncer wedged herself between a square shouldered silk suit and a fringe of glitter. A naughty giggle a rump shaking jiggle and she stepped into Act Two: A druggy blonde in fur and rocket heels stumbled to the center of the floor waving a revolver in her right hand. She fired three shots in the air. The crowd hushed and then panic set in under a woozy flood of orange neon. 'Baby I can make you feel good.'

Bouncer trapezed through the air.

Run!

Jump!

And with a flying side kick knocked the gun out of the woman's hand.

FEVER!

BLOOD!

The woman howled!

A scattershot of inaudible fuzz.

Her mouth hung open and a cocoon of red whammed the walls.

SEVEN RED

The Strand London
Monday 15th January 2001

Inside the Royal Courts of Justice, more particularly Court 13, Dempsey Loveitt was midway through his examination-in-chief. A tall silver-tongued truth twister with a halo of midnight gurl curls and thin sneery lips that often broke into a big devilish smile, he was both revered and reviled in equal measure by the sea of grey and blue pinstripe all around him. Loveitt spoke in that curdled arrogantly disdainful lawyer style with a weight and sharpness in his voice that made him sound superior to everyone else. "Members of the jury Oliver James Wainright is not a gangster, a porn merchant, kidnapper, murderer or smooth-talking conman. He is, however, an actor of the very highest caliber who has played all of these roles and many more besides, to great critical acclaim. Indeed with no less than five Oscar nominations, four Bafta wins and three Oliver awards, he is considered by many to be one of the very finest actors of his generation."

A slight pause. Loveitt stopped and cocked his head, staring attentively at the clack clack clack of the court stenographer's keyboard. Then he nodded at the usher and addressed the judge. "If it please your Lordship. Exhibit 72."

A crotchety voice underneath a fusty old wig and tippet ordered: "Proceed."

The jury were handed copies of a newspaper article with the banner headline *Wild Drug Orgy Ends in Tragedy*. Loveitt, a college trained Shakespearean actor, was adept at court room theatrics and thrived under the spotlight. He curled his thumbs round his gown and squared himself in front of the jury box.

"*The Daily Dispatch* would have you believe that Oliver James Wainright is a vile wicked man who dumped his wife and child in the middle of the Mojave Desert after a violent boozy drug-fuelled weekend. Page one paragraph three of this article highlighted in yellow for all to see is particularly pertinent. It reads inter alia, that Oliver James Wainright was a *public charmer and a private wife beater*. Alongside this revelation there is a somewhat blurry image of Mrs. Wainright's bruised and battered face and an ominous looking still photograph of Dante's View Death Valley, a premier tourist spot in the Mohave Desert. The photograph is dated with what appears to be a time stamp and accredited with the photographer's initials. L.K."

After an almighty, Pinteresque pause, Loveitt looked up as if he could hear false notes playing in the chamber of his mind and needed to rebalance them. Then with his big boomy voice he spoke into the deafening silence, so everyone had to stop what they were doing, and proclaimed, "Members of the jury every single one of these photographs is FAKE! Deliberately digitally doctored to ruin Mr. Wainright's reputation and ultimately destroy his career." Loveitt's bright mischievous eyes became two accusing money signs. "This entire story is a complete and shameful fabrication, intentionally orchestrated to depict Mr. Wainright as a nasty, odious, drunken, brute: drooling and stumbling around lost in his own deluded grandeur. A man who thinks only of himself and has a wanton disregard of everyone else." The jury sat spellbound, except for one pasty-faced jelly belly with blood red hair and a permanent scowl. Loveitt spied him through the corner of his eye, scribbling furiously on his notepad and stared hard at him through pauses, as he read out more salacious snippets from the article. "*After ingesting copious amounts of cocaine and a pint glass of whiskey, Mr. Wainright dragged his wife and six-year-old child into his Range Rover and sped off*… And there we have yet another distorted image of an allegedly inebriated Mr. Wainright, head slumped to the side, surrounded by what appears to be a vast array of drug paraphernalia."

All revved up, Loveitt let his reading glasses slide off his nose then waggled his finger at the jury, focusing on the red-headed man. "Members of the jury this is all a sham. Pure fiction. Mr. Wainright and his family were five thousand miles away in their London home when this story broke and categorically deny any of these events ever took place."

A change of tone, Loveitt's voice became courtly and didactic. "Members of the jury false images like these can spread from Milwaukee to Moscow, within seconds." He snapped his fingers angrily. "And just like that a viral news story is born without a scintilla of truth in it. These particular images were shared, disseminated, and reproduced on a colossal scale, via social media, word of mouth, and websites all over the world wide web, rolling news streams, and countless of other platforms, as well as on mainstream TV and both digital and analogue radio. The same lies repeated ad nauseum, over and over again, causing extreme hurt, embarrassment, and distress." He paced a little to the right, his index finger resting on his chin. "Indeed, picture trickery of this type is not new, but fortunately we can now test the veracity of these images and establish their provenance with the very same technology used to create them." A wolfish sneer spread across his face as he pulled out a glossy black and white photo from the trial bundle and expounded: "This is the picture of Mrs. Wainright that appears to show bruising to the eye and lacerations on the right cheek with a graze to the forehead. Page 82 of the bundle Exhibit 81 if you wish to follow along." He then pulled out three other glossies from the file and like a magician revealing the intricacies of a complicated trick, explained. "It was created by splicing two pictures together and superimposing the face of Mrs.

Wainright with a photoshopped publicity photo of her, used in an ad campaign for domestic abuse victims. These staged photographs were taken over a year ago." He looked up with a triumphant glow. "Pages 83 and 84 My Lord, Exhibits 81 a and b."

The court was hushed into silence. Now, Loveitt had every member of the jury eating from the palm of his hand. "You must have all heard of that delightful phrase a picture is worth a thousand words. We know Henrik Ibsen, Leonardo Davinci and Napoleon himself all laid claim to this popular proverb, and it still resonates today. Except, in this case, members of the jury just one of these doctored pictures is worth millions in revenue sales to *The Daily Dispatch*, and millions, in lost earnings and future earnings to Mr. Wainwright." Loveitt's tone, now doomsday urgent: "Members of the jury tabloid tinkering with celebrity photographs is not harmless fun. It can cost serious money and, on occasion, result in the victims losing their livelihoods, their relationships and ultimately their self-worth."

He shook his head ruefully. "A name. What is in a name? For Oliver James Wainright it is not only a question of his honour, his integrity, and his dignity. But his name, members of the jury, is his primary asset and to denigrate it, defame it, and drag it through the mud without just cause or good reason is akin to DESTROYING his very being. Let all the suns of the world burn me to ashes but let no stain tarnish my name."

The judge muffled a snigger, but a pert sunny-eyed juror in the front row seemed smitten. Loveitt bent down to tie the laces of his black rocker boots, a deliberate ploy to let his words sting the air.

Pennypick made an equally deliberate loud sigh and muttered angrily, "What a showman!"

Loveitt curled his mouth in distaste. "Shopping fake stories and fake pictures to an unsuspecting public is a rotten false flag manoeuvre, but one that generates new readers, new subscribers and supremely healthy profit margins. On publication of this specific fake story, sales figures for *The Daily Dispatch* tripled. Yes tripled. And it became the number one trending topic on all multimedia platforms." He looked down and rifled through a big bundle of papers at speed. "Page 82 My Lord shows detailed statistical data in exhibit 85."

He then trotted out various other technical methods deployed by the newspaper to create the misleading images and offered a logical forensic overview of how image manipulation and doctored pictures, when created with the express approval and complicity of a newspaper editor, was not only unjust, unfair, and inaccurate, but in breach of the Press Complaints Code. With operatic gusto and the heft and charm of a leading cinematic hero, he spoke at length about truth and justice. "Members of the jury I know I can rely upon you to bring that celestial virgin TRUTH down from her gilded throne and shower the court with her light." The red-headed dweeb looked sanctimonious.

The judge cleared his throat. "If we can move things along Mr. Loveitt. There'll be plenty of time for all of that in summary."

"Very well. M'Lord."

Loveitt's solicitor pulled at his gown then frantically passed him a note. He gave it a quick read then folded it neatly in half and stashed it away in his trouser pocket. He nodded purposefully at the judge then stared thoughtfully in the distance not giving anything away. A few seconds later, once the clock struck twelve, came the sensational smoking-gun moment. "Members of the jury what you're about to hear is part of a tape recording between the editor of *The Daily Dispatch,* one Robert Aloysious Rattlewort, and Mr. Wainright's film agent, Troy Havers. It conclusively proves that Mr. Rattlewort has a personal grudge against Mr. Wainright and was primarily activated by malice when he ordered this defamatory article to be published, intentionally using his newspaper to harass, intimidate and ultimately ruin Mr. Wainright's career."

Pennypick sprang to his feet. "Objection. My Lord this wasn't agreed." A thin over-literate weasel with an expensive tan and perfect teeth, he did his best to exclude the recording and prevent the jury from hearing it, but after seventeen stinging minutes of legal wrangling ultimately failed.

Loveitt picked up his argument. "My Lord if this can formally be admitted into evidence as Exhibit 105." He turned towards the jury. "The recording shows Mr. Rattlewort was comfortable using his newspaper to settle scores with any enemies he may have had. I apologise in advance for the vulgarity of the language deployed by the speaker M'Lord. The Judge nodded. A smoky, old timey, gruff South London voice ricocheted off the walls. "I'm warning ya Troy don't make a fucking joke out of me. You muppet. You know what your boy Wainright was up to. Everyone knows. Saw 'im takin' the piss. Now if you don't tell that fucking wormy bastard to behave and rein it in I'll do it miself. And I'll make sure 'e doesn't misbehave again. You don't wanna fight me on this, Troy. Consider yourselves warned. It's disrespectful and if he don't back off, I'll fuck him every which way. Back front and sideways. Am I making myself clear?"

Pennypick grimaced. The back pew of the public gallery was in shock. The front, consisting mainly of law students, talented interns and well-scrubbed local reporters unable to squeeze themselves into the press gallery, were busy making notes. Loveitt's brain whirred noisily. He knew he was skating on thin ice when he trumped the other side with the audio clip, but it was dynamite, and he was confident now he'd convinced the jury the article was deliberately manufactured and clearly defamatory. One of Rattlewort's unofficial dangerous sidekicks was hovering at the back of the courtroom watching everything play out. The law clerk, a woman in her mid-thirties, smiled a secret smile. Once the recording stopped, Loveitt cracked his knuckles and waited. The judge looked around sourly and said, "Let's break for lunch. We'll reconvene at two p.m."

Loveitt sailed back to his office in sunny spirits, armed with a trolley of files, some handwritten scribbles of key points and his lucky charm dangling between his fingers. A small red horseshoe pricked with mini-diamonds that he carried on his keychain. His daughter had bought it for his fiftieth birthday, and he took it with him everywhere. He plonked his papers down and was surprised to see most of his fellow colleagues alongside the head of chambers, Jollyon Roberts Q.C., all huddled together in the first floor waiting room, glued to the main TV screen. The case was headline news, and there was an angry buzz about Rattlewort.

Roberts sidled up to Loveitt with a congratulatory slap on the back and friendly fist pump. "This is going to go nuclear. It's already the biggest story on all the news networks even Rattlewort's own channels! Guaranteed to be the lead story in the papers tomorrow. You better watch out. Things are going to be very different for you. Be ready." After a fizzy hour of smiles, a sneaky glass of champagne and a couple of lines of coke, Loveitt grabbed his wig and gown and headed out.

He decided to walk back to court for the afternoon session. His chambers were only a hop skip and jump away but he had a brief stop to make at the Cittie of York pub in Holborn. The more his mind wandered, the more he had this nagging feeling in his gut that he just couldn't shake. He knew it was a huge gamble having Rattlewort as an enemy, like a jackal out for a kill, lurking in the shadows just waiting for Loveitt to slip up.

It was a bright but bitterly cold day. The whip of the wind slapped his cheeks and ruffled his hair, and he had to shield his eyes from the sun's angry glare. Roadworks, pneumatic drills, the wail of ambulances and the screech of police sirens accompanied him on his short walk. A youngish street sleeper, her face washed with a dreamy ochre light, a broken-bird tilt to her head and eyes bigger than the Tower of London, seemed lost in her own fountain of misery. He stopped to offer her a little change, but she gently shooed him away. It rattled him. Confused, he crossed the road, and glanced back at her, but she was gone. He checked his watch. He still had thirty minutes left before court…

Once he'd cleared the metal detectors in the lobby, Loveitt bounded up the stairs to Court 13. He nodded politely at Pennypick and sat down. He was rummaging around for a pen, checked his inside jacket pocket, and instead found a crumpled yellow post-it note which read: *I SAW YOU* in big red threatening letters. He shoved it into his trouser pocket and bit his lip then glanced around nervously searching for answers. *Who saw what and how did that pesky little note get there*? As he waited for the judge and everyone else to return from lunch, he tried to hang onto that sunny feeling. He was on his way to victory, he'd already outfoxed Pennypick, and it would be a hard sell persuading the jury that the newspaper article was true; it was clearly libellous. If Rattlewort didn't want to come up with a reasonable settlement, then Loveitt was determined to make it as unpleasant as possible for him and his bully-boy wrecking crew inside the courtroom.

With everyone still waiting for the judge, a perfectly poised, high cheek-boned, sparkly pants popped her head around the courtroom door. She waved Loveitt over with a big wide smile. He strolled to the door full of curiosity. "Mr. Loveitt my name's Tiggy Birch I work for *Legal News* we'd love to do a feature on you for the show once the trial's over." She slipped him a business card and left.

Court was called into session and the afternoon zipped by, but there was definitely something odd going on with the defence. Pennypick was unusually cooperative and kept smiling at him. He had eased off on the objections too, including three key matters of evidence and made very little noise about other applications filed on behalf of Mr. Wainright. Loveitt felt very uneasy seeing Pennypick so relaxed about the case. He grew even more suspicious when after a short toilet break, he saw Rattlewort himself, having a heated conversation with the judge's clerk in the stairwell. The day ended with laughter when a ginger tabby sneaked into the courtroom with a coachload of Japanese tourists.

Loveitt raced back to chambers with a bad feeling. He needed to find out who wrote that note and wanted to go over some witness testimony. He worked solidly for four hours with no leads on the note but did perfect his oratory skills in front of a long line mirror and honed all of his arguments for cross examination.

Lounging on a bottle green Chesterfield, he took several calls. One was from a magazine that was covering the case. "My client will be victorious. Newspapers think they can print what they like with no comeback. I'm there drilling for the truth to protect my client's reputation and make the liars accountable. Yes, quote me."

He had a quick chat with his secretary and warned, "You know how it is. Celebrities can be really stupid. They have a way of exposing themselves and foolishly believe they can say anything, and that their fans will still adore them regardless. I don't think we'll put any of Wainright's showbiz chums on the stand. They could alienate the jury." His secretary, Harvinder Singh Dhillon, a tall, exquisitely mannered Sikh gent, with slicked electric blue turbaned hair and poetic eyes, nodded his understanding.

"Oh, and get me up an updated financial statement on the

Barstow case." Harvinder smiled in acquiescence and drifted out of the room.

Loveitt was about to grab a late dinner when his mobile phone bleeped. He didn't recognize the number, and it was too late for diverted office calls. He picked up cautiously.

"Dempsey Loveitt speaking how can I help?"

A soft strangulated voice. He couldn't make out if it was a female voice or a high-pitched male one, but there was something oddly familiar about it.

"How are you Loveitt?"

"Sorry, who is this? I didn't catch a..."

The caller cut in impatiently. "That's because I didn't give you my name. I asked you a question and I'd be obliged if you answered it."

Loveitt took a sip of cold coffee. "Who is this?"

"Meet me inside 174 Blackfriars Bridge and I'll give you a little reminder. If you want to finally get off the ledge, you'll be there in an hour."

The caller clicked off, and Loveitt sat stewing for a few minutes. He wasn't unduly worried, just concerned. *What did all that jiggery pokery mean? What ledge who what why where...* the questions were piling up. He checked his work emails and text messages when suddenly he remembered that voice. Like a sharp burn on his conscience. He opened the door to his safe and pulled out a soft grey pouch, a large brown envelope and a wad of cash. Inside the pouch, a semi-automatic Berretta M9. He took it and traced his finger around the end of the barrel, then placed both the gun and the envelope in his backpack and pocketed the cash.

Instinctively he started frantically shredding bits of paper and old documents. He made a bank transfer to an off shore account in Belize and offloaded some gold stock online. He was already putting on his coat when one of the work placement trainees, Natasha Ofili, cornered him at the door.

She was halfway through her mini pupillage and had that boundless enthusiasm and youthful naivete that Loveitt thrived on. "I'm so sorry to disturb you, I was just wondering if I could shadow you at court tomorrow."

The steady whirr of the paper shredder could be heard in the background. She bustled inside and saw Loveitt's lucky horseshoe on the desk pointing downwards. She looked at it quizzically. "Um isn't this meant to be facing up?"

"What?"

"The horseshoe, you know, the legend of St. Dunstan?"

Loveitt stared at her blankly.

"According to the legend, the devil demanded Dunstan, who was a blacksmith, to shoe his horse, but Dunstan nailed it in the devil's hoof instead, only agreeing to remove it if the devil stayed away from anyone who had a horseshoe. But in order for the pact to work, all seven points have to be facing up so that the shoe can fill up with good luck."

Loveitt feigned politeness. "Fascinating." Then ushered her out with a smile. "Now don't be late see you at nine thirty sharp in the Beer Garden."

She waved goodbye, and finally Loveitt was left alone. For a moment he just sat there in glassy silence staring at the wall. He toyed with lots of variables in the forest of his mind. *How can you just leave all of the dirt and dissolve into the citadel of pampered white truffles. You can't. Eventually over time you become part of the dirt.* He paused and looked around his office, admiring the provocative art: two floating heads, suspended above a pink cloudless sky, the old, framed certificates and diplomas that hung so proudly on the left wall and his big, chipped antique desk. That's where his real power lay, in every crack and scratch under the mound of papers, books, and files. Once he had wanted to be part of that legal razzle dazzle, that hallowed institution. Once he was awed by their quirky traditions and fabled history. Now he understood better. And for a moment all the misery of middle-class shame was caged in the lines on his face.

He scrambled out to black restless skies, hurrying through a maze of side streets and little alleyways. They were filling up with a kind of vivant tableau of night crawlers: sugar-bombed sex workers wrapped in lurex and shiny boob tubes, junkies looking for golden highs, pimps on the prowl, young girls in skinny-stretch-denim, gawping at an X-rated world in-between mouthfuls of Haagen-Dazs, and skipping to the latest beats. It was all so familiar to Loveitt and touched a soft spot. *Misfits, drunks and mystics.* This gluey wasteland of pizza crusts, used condoms, phlegm, discarded bullets of nitrous gas and dead balloons of smashed dreams was an entire world away from his cosy bourgeois sanctum of legal privilege. *All it takes is one wrong turn, one mistake.*

He lit a Marlboro and listened to the dirty rhythms of the night. After several short puffs he tossed it aside and continued east towards Blackfriars Bridge. When he came to the underpass behind a fenced patch of grass and planks of rotting plywood, he looked above as rows of twinkly lights streamed across the Thames, the ageless cosmo-chic crowd giggling the night away in sunny luxury on pricey Chablis and glasses of Prosecco.

Lost in the labyrinth of his mind, Loveitt knew the judge, the street sleeper, the clerk and Rattlewort's sidekick were all just pawns in a bigger game. Wary of the jackal off in the shadows—or a raven-headed viper with something sharp.

They splashed a banner headline in *The Daily Dispatch*, the lawyer and his lucky red horseshoe.

THE END

HORIZONTAL VERTICAL

A low swung smile on her heart-shaped face. Half-naked-topless in bordello-red panties. Her left leg slung at a ninety-degree angle across a black scrunched cocktail dress. Her right leg straddled the arm of an easy-fit budget sofa upholstered in an aggressive shade of convict orange. On the floor beside her, an open tub of vaginal jelly, three fingers of blow and a dinky gold-plated cocaine spoon. It was noon. The sun vomiting diluted rays of insipid light into the room. A slit of dust on the coffee table and a shit-strewn kitty litter box sat by the back wall. It stunk of broken promises. Kiki Loveheart aka Mizz WhipKink aka Maddie Summers aka Sweet Cheeks 69. Kreative Gig artiste and professional cat sitter. Eking out a piece meal existence as: Daytime nurse - afternoon phone sex operator - night crawling glamour queen and private stripper.

Forced to juggle four jobs just to live in a cramped, foul-smelling, roach-ridden walk up. She stared ruefully at her purple lizard leather stilettos. She felt like a *Penthouse* pin up in those heels. They elongated her calf muscles popped her pelvis and kinked her hips. Strutting the sidewalk never felt so good. Kiki blinked, yawned, and slowly got up. Barefoot. She tip-toed to the refrigerator and took out a cold bottle of San Pellegrino and rolled it against her forehead.

"Ahh."

"Keeeeeki?"

A goopy taffy-laced little voice. It could have belonged to a third grader or a whiny half-bagged grandma but it belonged to Michael Wiesel. A squiffy-eyed Buddha-faced eight- toed high-talking sex *perv.* Serial fraudster, bourgeois rapist and TV Judge. Presiding over his own primetime TV show, that pitted litigants in person against one another. Miserable little suburban dramas. Scripted for mass consumption.

Of course, it was a ratings winner and Wiesel wore his success like an electric lit billboard. His patterned argyle socks, vintage Rolex, silk-satin tux and two-ply cotton designer shirt screamed smug money. But his ageing blond-comb over pomaded across his jutting forehead, swollen bucket-gut and peeling pink skin humbled him on occasions, especially at funerals, country clubs, and IRS meetings.

"Keeeeeki. C'meer. I want chou to freshen up. Put on a dress or somethin' pretty. You look like a syphilitic ghetto slut. Clean yaw self-up. Dirty bitch."

His accent pure New Yawk. Purple gums on show. He threw a couple of c-notes on the floor and flashed his platinum-circled pinkie. Loose-lipped pig mouth slapped her butt with another slew of insults: "You need a tan – lose a few pounds – I like your hair straight - classy chicks wear perfume - get bigger tits."

Twenty-eight years old and still listening to fruitless fuck balls who reminded her that she was just a split-second vignette in THE BIG PICTURE. She switched her gaze between a moldy slice of Kraft deli-deluxe and Wiesel's spreading bald spot. Swirling her tongue around her index finger, she whispered. "Got a better idea."

"Yeah?"

"Hmmmm. Why don't I text Nahhhtashhha? And we mix it up." Natashaar: Twentyish. Nouveau redhead. Faux Russian accent big bazookas - shapely ass - creamy lips. Sweeter than Nutella and Kiki's bestie. The pair of them responsible for a rash of tricks that would make even the hardest hustler blush.

"Whaddya have in mind?"

"Wait and see."

"Do it."

"Okayyyyy. Make yourself more comfortable. Take off your pants."

Kiki grabbed her phone from the dresser. Natasha would be there in a few minutes. Wiesel was caught between the bastard of time and his own carnal greed. He paced the floor like a restless tiger. "Hurry up."

"She won't be long. Relax. Sit down. C'mon."

She patted the seat with a fiendish glint in her eye. Then slid on thigh-scraper black velvet boots and a black leather string bikini. Wiesel's creeper peepers fixed on her downy v-shape mound peeping through the slit of her gusset.

Kiki hissed, "This really is ground zero of the Walmart sex trade. Puny limp dick with big dick complex. Today I'm jumping off that pyramid."

"Whaddya say. Speak up?"

"I said you know you make me so hot for it."

The creases on Wiesel's face were lined with dust and type 2 diabetic sweat.

Everything Kiki did to make things better slam-jammed into nothing and now here she was, star of her own dime-store noir. Her mind somersaulted at freeway speed: *Cancer-table sex - a black swan - yogi-tea homilies - dead-sister cancer be yourself shaman mantras - truck stop suicides - cancer blue- rubber covered asses - booby-trapped commitment - rib eye steak pus-filled promises - Je Je Spa Happy Ending Massage Kung Fu nuns Himalayas auto-erotic strangulation.*

Squatting on a throne of debt. Kiki was tired of sleazo tricksters. Tired of renting herself out to small-souled roly poly hardballs. Tired of one bowl - easy mac frozen dinners-three-minute hustles with teenage dopers and cheapo plastic heart break. Her brain backed up with years of toxic yesterdays. Ever since her only sister had succumbed to cancer. She felt trapped in a psycho blizzard. She wanted out.

Wiesel. He was the catalyst. Sprawled there. On her green linoleum five-dollar armchair. Balancing papers on his balloon shaped stomach. Tapping his foot to an invisible beat. Kiki stiffened. The double thump of her heart jumped three seconds. She had a driving primal urge to glass him in the neck, and played every move slowly, in the dungeon of her mind. *Psych out!*

It wasn't the most original way to kill someone, but it was definitely doable. It made her body tingle. She knew that Wiesel kept at least 10 grand in his grab bag. A pre-packed emergency kit stocked with doomsday end of the world shit. Wiesel carried it everywhere he went. Bragging to anyone who'd listen that he was ready for Armageddon. It was the perfect get away bag. Ideal for two huzzies on the lam. Kiki's murder plan simmering in the cauldron of her mind. Something gross and a little immoral was about to happen.

"Ding dong ding ding dong."

"That'll be Natassha."

Kiki buzzed her up. Wiesel moistened his mouth and moved to the bed. Panting his fairy tale sex romp through Pepto Bismol coughs. Natasha bounced into view. "Well, hellllloooo! How ya doing?"

Rude-cute in a stylized red plaid mini, cropped shirt, white gartered knee highs a striped tie with pigtailed hair and cheap Mary Jane shoes. She slow-kissed Kiki and cupped her face in her hands. Wiesel unbuttoned his shirt, revealing an expanse of silver and brown gorilla chest hair and a thatch of wispy fuzz that sprung from the nape of his neck. He stank of onions and tuxedoed fraud.

Tracking the curves of Kiki's thighs, he said, "You know what I love about your type?"

Natasha pulled away grinning. "Our type?"

"Yeah, pussy princesses."

Kiki's eyes narrowed. "What?"

He ignored the sarcastic inflexion in her voice and sucked his teeth. "You understand that sex is just a business. I don't have to think too hard. I fuck you. Pay you: You're mine."

His mildew eyes clung to her ass. She had to dig her nails in her palms to stop herself from puking in his lap. In a bitter-sweet tone, part Marilyn Monroe, part Morticia Adams, she whispered: "Let's try something new."

A dangerous smile curled her lips. Together they cuffed Wiesel to the bed. Kiki placed a blindfold on his eyes.

"C'mon -let's get on with it." He growled.

Kiki and Natasha shared a knowing wink. Natasha banged her hips in Wiesel's face. Toying with him while Kiki got busy.

"You think you know our type? Think again!"

"Aaaaaaaargh!"

She gagged him with a pair of sheer stockings. Deaf to his protestations. The gentle curve of her mouth promised more pain. Natasha bound his ankles with bondage tape and leather restraints.

Kiki steamed. "It's you and *your* type. You're the limp dick asshole who's got your greedy cheating hands all over the city. Everybody knows you're as crooked as hell. We're the only ones hurting."

Kiki marched into the kitchenette. Smashed the bottle against the wall and stomped back to the bedroom. She ignored the little yelps, and spittle, dribbling down Wiesel's chin. Now he was thrashing around like a bottom-trawled fish gasping for air. Kiki gripped the base of the bottle, jabbed it into his neck, and sliced open his throat, hitting both carotid arteries and his jugular.

Blood rhymes splattered the sheets.

They racked up the balance of the coke, Kiki armed with the grab bag. "C'mon let's get outta here."

A few moments of thin silence. Kiki's voice strangely alien eaten by the shadows in the room:

"*Ghetto sluts* like me, always end up vertical not horizontal."

THE END

PROFIT AND LOSS (A LONDON STORY)

The glitzy eye of the capital dimmed by savage wage cuts, job losses, unlicensed pawn shops, rampant racism, and those overfed piggy bankers. 5:00 am underneath Waterloo Station: Empty cans of Stella-KFC chicken boxes, and orphaned, pound store socks lay strewn across the mouth of the underpass. It stunk of skunk--sick man's urine and a hungry bull mastiff.

Sitting on a crinkled grocery bag: Ginger, a streaky- haired, seventeen-year-old petal of light stretched her arms out. Former stage school flunkey and forgotten insta star, now part-time flower arranger and full-time coke addict. Defiant in charity couture. She was all trussed up in lime green spandex, a red polyester mini-skirt, and sheer stockings mottled with runs. A beige rain mac and a pair of three-inch black plastic stilettos lay neatly by her side. Sodium vapor lights painted yellowy stripes across her elfin face and made her skin pop with an ethereal phantom-like tint. She looked like a wild extra-terrestrial flower from a sci-fi flick. Her smoke-coloured eyes flashing violently when a lanky, pony- tailed rake slumped in front of her. He wore baggy, bleached denim, a porkpie hat, and a drab-green sweatshirt. His feet covered by bird-shitted trainers splattered with months of missed opportunities, bad luck, and hard-nosed rejection. Ichabod Funk (Ich). Homeless. Music school dropout, occasional post-literate poet and street-scammer. Ich trotted around selling stolen crap, mostly useless intel, and mobile phone sim cards. With his big shiny expectant eyes and childlike view of the world he was waiting for a miracle or something. His shattered dream of becoming 'someone', shredded in the excrement of social cleansing. Still strictly small-time he had stumbled on a Baudelairean hangout, The Horseshoe, a few miles away in Portobello Road. His pinched nasal voice overridden by a see-saw lilt made him sound like Ringo Starr from the Beatles only with a London twang.

"We gotta go. C'mon."

Ginger looked at him sourly.

"It took me five hours to get this space." She spoke in a muted tone. The frost-tipped tongue of December had licked her fingers raw and it was a struggle for her to get the words out.

"I have a place for us to go. C'mon."

Ich gathered up the rain-stained lightweight duvet, sample-sized toiletries and a half-drunk bottle of Pepsi. Everything they owned, hurriedly packed away in disposable black garbage bags. Ginger dumped the cardboard sheets and Milky Way wrappers. They were always on the move. Like a never-ending story played in real time with no final chapter in sight. Most of their days were spent stalking shop doorways and empty benches for a spot to rest. A new government initiative meant that almost every single public bench and store exit they stumbled across was now blocked by an ugly slew of spiked barriers. Erected steel fangs deliberately positioned over warm air vents to stop them snatching even a few minutes of precious sleep. Ginger thought it amounted to state sponsored cruelty. A sharp and constant reminder of their *HOMELESS* status.

Ginger's eyes danced from mad to menacing. Attacked by a nest of erratic cocaine-fueled thoughts, she opened the bowels of her mind as she watched a sequin of sparkly partygoers slink by: *Pretty long-haired bitches with your bottled tans talking - titties singing assess and fake eyelashes - judging me with pouty lip disgust I had a life too once upon a time and who are you to judge if I shove my fist in your satin-glossed mouth. Are you gonna scream and shout? Sometimes I can't change my tampon for days. Sometimes I wipe the dried blood off with my little finger. And all I can eat is stale cheeseburgers micro-flipped for a minute or rotting scraps from the trash. Will I wake up dead? Just another statistic in an unmarked grave. You look at me like I'm a slimy-back -sliding spider - struggling to climb outta a sink hole. I got big dreams - just ask the angels. Ask them if I'd be forgiven for stabbing you in the throat. If I could wash my fingers in warm peachy soap and not the public scum-furred toilets where that sex perv with lice in his beard masturbates in front of me while I'm trying to take a dump. Righteous reformers! With your patronizing 'healing' smirks. You make me puke offering me free lattes while I crawl around in the dirt. I'm just a way for you to bag likes and shares as you take another pic for your growing twitter feed. Here's one for your Majesty! So beloved of gushy American tourists and the English middle classes. Why am I the outsider? And why are you ENTITLED to shit on me and plant your royal arses on acres of land without worrying about paying the tax man? The poisoned parasitic slurp of the English Monarchy fucks us all. What kind of sicko world is this where hordes of people stand in line to catch a glimpse of your smug little face and grovel at your feet begging to shake your grasping white-gloved hand? You're not Jesus Christ and you didn't cure cancer!*

Ginger's intestines were angry. Her sore swollen stomach wept as she stuttered her way out of the hallowed sleep-spot tugging at Ich's sleeve while he carted their belongings on his back.

"They treat us like infected - diseased - vermin. Less than human. Even stray dogs and cats can get a pat on the head and a warm bed for the night."

Ich frowned.

"Please don't worry. We're gonna be fine. We're going to The Horseshoe. Someone's going to help us out."

"Who?"

"You'll see."

They trudged through a maze of jagged back streets and alleyways. Wet half-moon sweat rings circled Ginger's sleeves, so she pinged the elastic at the top of her leotard and tried to air her unwashed body. They passed a roly-poly middle-aged woman with a pink bandana on her head, her voice thick with indignation: "They're raping intelligence with money..."

Ginger nodded sympathetically then turned to Ich.

"Do you think we'll always be living like this? I feel like my soul's choking."

Ich marched on without listening. Ginger continued her semi-coherent aria of anguish. Her voice got louder and more desperate. "It's like a long-broken ladder to nowhere. I've climbed thousands of steps every day looking for one tiny penny of hope."

And that's what she feared the most, that she'd never find HOPE. That golden kiss of survival everybody needs to hang on to.

She pretended they were renegades bouncing through the streets in shimmery non-conformist splendor but then life would invariably stand up on its hind legs and slap her on the arse.

Sometimes Ginger thought about life before her mother died. She would close her eyes and let her mother's voice float inside her. It reminded her of a tiny burst of sunlight and cherry vanilla ice cream. Mostly it reminded her of a way out. But that feeling didn't last long and her daily tableau of survival always dragged her back to the moment.

6.00 am. The skies were reddening like a Boschian/Hirst mash up. They were still a few minutes away. They slipped past a passel of unknown arty types noodling around on the edge of insanity, and a slouch of elderly junkies clumped together for their graveyard fix. Ginger saw one of them toying with a switchblade. She flinched and hurried after Ich. Finally, they arrived outside a narrow nondescript building with a U-shaped doorway. Ich led them inside. The bar was empty save for some sorry slacks at the back, a thin-boned Chinese barman and a corner table flanked by three refrigerator-sized, sober-suited baldies.

In front of them surrounded by a trip of hostile looking misfits sat a small, slithery looking man: Zipmouth.

Almost dapper in a custom-made navy checked suit and cream button-down shirt. A shock of cinematic bouffant silver curls framed his huge walnut-sized menacing eyes. De rigeur St. Barts tan set off a strong hawk nose, and thick mutton chop sideburns. But nothing could prepare them for that ear-to- mouth slash; a misshapen zip-stitched mouth GASH. It was the kind of visceral *Freddy Krueger* moment that stretched from your eyes and stayed in your stomach for weeks.

Ginger squirmed. Ich kept perfectly still.

A slim beach bunny blonde was perched on Zipmouth's lap. Even sitting she was a good head taller than him. His voice was activated by a mechanized electro throat-back. A hand-held battery powered device used by people who'd lost their voice box. He pushed the blonde aside and motioned Ich and Ginger closer. An American-accented tinny robotic voice sliced the air. Stephen Hawking style: "Come. Here. Let. Me. See. You."

Ich dropped the bags and folded his palm around Ginger's paper-thin wrist. Slowly they walked towards the table. The three heavies stood aside.

"I'll. Get. Straight. To. The. Point. I can see you're in need."

Ginger winced. A sharp intake of breath. She tried her best not to stare at Zipmouth's lopsided jaw. But she seemed fascinated by it. Ich squeezed her hand and she changed focus, concentrating on Zipmouth's eyes. Two red-rimmed slits. As he leant forward, she noticed a floppy strip of wattled skin dangling from his chin. It reminded her a little of a shop-soiled Christmas turkey.

"Ichabod. It's. Time. To. Think. Big. To-mo-rrow. My. Crew are int-ter-cepting an electronic cash transfer from Wonga Wonga Bank. We need you to create a diversion inside. We have clothes and disguises. You'll be given details and paid after the job. Any questions?"

Neither of them felt they had the right to ask any questions.

"Good. Have a little fun on me." He handed Ich half a dozen red disc-shaped pills embossed with a skull and crossbones. Ich popped one straight away. Ginger slipped a couple in her pocket for later. Zipmouth ended the conversation casually.

"See. You. Kids. Around. Sharkie has everything you need."

He pointed at a pigeon-nosed lummox dressed in a nylon jogging suit who escorted them out. Sharkie trashed their belongings in a nearby dumpster and handed them a shiny new case of mixed apparel. Ginger wondered if they got her size right. Sharkie chauffeured them to a discreet gated apartment in Central London. A satin wrapped paradise. They entered the lux hideout with a mixture of awe and excitement and silently waved goodbye to the grey bony glaze of London grime. Sharkie left a few minutes later with instructions to be up before noon.

On the table in the main room, a bouquet of assorted fresh flowers, gift wrapped candies and a generous basket of seasonal fruit. A state of the art high-res plasma screen hung on the wall in isolated glory and underneath it a built-in desk and fully stocked mini-bar. Ginger squealed like a hamster hopped up on molly and clapped her hands over her mouth in disbelief: "What the fuck is going on? This is like some *Bond* bollocks or some other freaky shit. Who WAZ that guy? Did you see his mouth? Jeeezus. Really fucking freaky. And how -

how did *you* do this?" She waltzed around from room to room dazed by nouveau comforts, periodically erupting into fits of giggles. A small kitchenette stuffed with snacks pre-packed meats soft drinks and vegetables proved too much of a temptation. Ginger helped herself to fun-sized chocolate bars and gourmet potato chips then threw off her plastic heels. In-between mouthfuls, she fumbled around for the little red pills and washed them down with a can of Red Bull. Then she flopped herself on the bed. A queen-sized double-deluxe. She felt the pristine line of the sheets between her thumb and forefinger and buried her face in the soft fluffy covers. Plumping the pillows, she bounced up and down on the mattress.

Ich was quiet. Almost sullen. He sat down cross-legged on the floor, just staring weirdly at nothing. Ginger made a beeline for the bathroom. Hurriedly she stripped off and filled the tub with lavender scented foam. Frothing around in complimentary bubbles she grabbed the shower head using it as a makeshift mic radiating liquid joy as she lathered up. "Your love is king…" She cooed.

In the lounge Ich popped two more pills. Then he lit a cigarette and took a deep drag.

On the other side of London, Zipmouth: Fixer, trafficker and organ harvester was briefing his small clique of cutthroat body snatchers. Getting them ready to prowl the city looking for fresh blood. Paid to find potential "donors", for a myriad of medical procedures. Of course, you couldn't just pop body organs out. Zipmouth's recruits had a tried and tested method involving one whack to the head and a potentially fatal dose of morphine or fentanyl. Earlier that week he had already met with a high-ranking administrator at an exclusive London hospital and had created a stack of forged consent forms and death certificates to validate donation. With a select medical team, private ambulance, and a dozen obscenely rich patients on standby, the wheezy cackly hissy smelly, panting demon of GREED was Ready. To. Kill.

Transplant tourism, once a thriving black-market economy limited to China, India, and West Africa, had gone global. The spike in world diseases meant there was now an unprecedented demand for replacement body parts. Zipmouth liked to squeeze as much as he could out of a deal. Hearts lungs and livers were all hot properties, but kidneys were the most prized on the black market. Zipmouth could get as much as eighty thousand pounds for just one. He preferred harvesting kidneys as they were generally easy to remove without too many complications. He attempted a smile. His liver-spotted mitt clicked the electro larynx. Blue-veined money fingers on show.

"Thank. God. For. Heart disease high blood pressure and diabetes."

10.00 am: At the apartment. Ich and Ginger were lost in eternal slumber. Their bodies entwined. Their faces inches apart. Ginger's freshly washed locks braided with the golden tipped fingers of the sun. Her lips half parted like a tulip in bloom. A look of utter relief on her face.

THE END

LA VENGEANCE DE LEO

Chi Chi was a petty dope dealer full-time fraudster and occasional paralegal. She had frittered away all of her meagre inheritance on footwear and frivolous froth like French designer jeans and lacy bedroom panties. Karl used to say she was a "poster pinup for the bourgeoisie." They broke up when she sold his flamenco guitar on e-bay and she fucked his best friend in the Café Rouge parking lot. She told him while they were watching a Netflix miniseries on sociopaths. She remembered his big sad eyes like two accusing dollar signs.

Midnight at Klub 7: Chi Chi tried to block a platoon of dark thoughts from clouding her mind as she double-stepped her way to the bar and sat down next to a flirty old buzzard with a sexy gold tooth and a sunny laugh. She slipped off her jacket and struck a voguish pose. Hot Americano legs stole the limelight.

"Can I get you a drink?"

"Why thank you very much…"

"You can call me Bob."

His voice reminded her of scratchy nettles.

"I'll have a rum and coke Bob."

The barkeep sailed in from nowhere, topped up Bob's glass, and set hers on the counter.

Chi Chi spied the hands of opportunity crawl through the twinkle of Bob's eyes.

"You're sneaky. You look like trouble with a capital T."

She threw her head back and laughed and it was like uncorking a bottle of champagne. "All my friends call me Chi Chi."

Bob chuckled. "You really know how to bust those moves. I'm like a constipated racoon out there."

"Ah there's nothing to it you just jiggle and jive. Somehow it all comes together."

Two whiskey-bombed hours later Chi Chi slunk into Bob's exclusive beach hideaway. And when she stripped off, they became two frolicking waves in the ocean of the night.

Around 3:00 a.m. Chi Chi woke up. She could smell the drift of Johnnie Walker on Bob's grizzled face. She looked around in wonder. It was like a show house. Straight out of *Harper's Bazaar*. Her silent smile spread into a grin. She stared at Bob and his curb stone skin all grey and scaly like a map of unfinished endings.

There were all the signs of a big-ticket life but as she tiptoed around, she knew something was off. She couldn't decide if the chemi-trails in her brain were playing cheap tricks on her or if she'd really heard her mother's voice.

Why?

She dug her nails deep into her palms to stop herself from crying.

Mamma? Mamma? Where are you?

Suddenly she felt a cold rush of air. Her nipples hardened. She crept back to bed and laid back down next to Bob. His throat hummed as he turned his body towards her. A sweaty tangle of strangeness and comfort.

She slept until noon. There was a yellow post it-note on the dresser. It read: *Help yourself to champagne and eggs Bob xo.* She hopped out of bed and floated into the kitchen. A vulgar smack of culinary porn. Big beamed ceilings and the ubiquitous standalone island. The refrigerator, a sleek stainless armoire of greedy decadence, ate up two thirds of the room. Slowly she opened the door. Apart from all the crushed ice and luxe gourmet fare she spied a delicate black box pitted with air holes sitting on the middle shelf. She picked it up and turned it over. *Probably a fancy schmancy block of cheese or something a little more exotic.*

She held it close to her ear and listened. It sounded like the chatter of old men praying; A spiritual mantra of some kind. Ya be Yae. Ya be Yae. A wave of disorientation and a scattering of stinging light. Terrified, Chi Chi dropped the box and on impulse scrambled for the door. She had a tight dry feeling in her throat. Her eyes dimmed and the last thing she saw was a fury of red ants dancing around her ankles as she collapsed onto the cold terracotta tiles.

When she finally woke up a slap of green neon enveloped her. It covered the walls, the ceiling and the barrel of a Glock 43 inches away from her head. She gulped and stole a breath.

This can't be real… in her mind she rationalised a neo Lynchian film of distraction. Soon the three-foot talking blue haired munchkins would bounce into view and she could catch up on some well needed sleep. But instead, she was confronted with the lurid shadow of a woman. Her face hidden by a creepy theatre mask with the eyes and mouth hollowed out. One side tragedy the other comedy.

"Chi Chi. Even that name sounds fake. Like a cutesy liddle Pomeranian or one of those tacky cocktails. You know with a paper umbrella sticking out the top. Either way, it's so… you."

There was something eerily familiar about that greying voice. A voice sharpened with hate and Pepto Bismol.

"This is a beautiful place eh?"

She nodded and tried to squint away all the sickly green. "I don't understand… who...?"

The woman laughed through her mask. "You were always trying to be niceeee. So nice."

"Please. I… where's Bob?"

The woman slithered closer and laid her gloved palm across Chi Chi's cheek.

Chi Chi flinched and tried to back away, but she was hemmed in from all sides. *Could that be Bob's wife or…*

A brief queasy silence.

"Who are you what do you want from me?"

"Now that's a start. That's what I expect from a wannabe lawyer."

The woman slipped off her mask with theatrical panache. "Now do you remember?"

Her face was a complex trail of unhappy yesterdays.

Chi Chi could see all the misery of the world kettled in that face.

She tried to place her but all she could think of was Swedish fish and milk balls. Her stomach grumbled as she let out a short sigh.

The woman grinned and revealed a mushy purple gum line. "You left me with nothing. I should have been sipping Mai Tai's on Coco Beach. But here I am working as a maid for Bob. On my hands and knees scrubbing his toilet clean. Mopping up dog piss. Washing walls, clearing cupboards, and waiting..." She shook her head. "Rich people can be so funny. They'll spend four million on a house and buy a cheap vacuum for twenty bucks. Go figure."

A sarcastic laugh. "As for me I get just enough to keep my Fico score alive and a stack of pancakes at Denny's every Friday."

She narrowed her eyes right down to two sharpened red slits. "I've been trailing your cheating ass for months. Just waiting and waiting for my chance. Then fate came knocking… and in a stroke of synchronicity well, here we are."

A tea-coloured wheeze landed on Chi Chi's thigh.

Chi Chi flashed back to a sunny day in June. Elizabeth Rawlins, a sixty-five-year-old widow, had walked into the office and trusted her with every penny she had. And now a year ago to the day Chi Chi aka Cameron Bell sat face to face with her conscience.

Mrs. Rawlins had a surprisingly steady hand, but her voice was shaky. "When you forged the deeds to my house and stole it from me, they burnt it to the ground. Leo was inside."

Chi Chi's lips tightened.

Mrs. Rawlins started to sob. "Leo was more than just a cat. He was… family."

She didn't think the old woman would do it, couldn't believe she was capable of pulling the trigger but that weird light in Mrs. Rawlins eyes unsettled her.

Chi Chi screeched and jumped towards her. Mrs. Rawlins toppled backwards and dropped the gun. Chi Chi made a scramble for the stairs but tripped on the third one. Mrs. Rawlins limped forward, grabbed her ankles and tried to drag her back. "I'm gonna use every last breath…"

Chi Chi kicked her away, crawled to the top of the stairs, unbolted the front door, and ran…

Mrs Rawlins gathered herself together and left the apartment clutching Chi Chi's smashed ankle chain. On her way home she felt a gravitational pull on her energy and immediately dialed Maryanne, a practicing witch. For the next few days, Mrs. Rawlins immersed herself in magic rituals with Maryanne, mostly involving the sacrificial slaughter of dead mice, dead pigeons and Chi Chi's broken ankle chain. They made little paper aeroplanes and wrote their wishes on them. Mrs. Rawlins spat on hers then they released them into the East River.

Baja Mexico

Chi Chi sat alone sipping a Mai Tai cocktail watching the ruby crown of the sun sink beneath restless skies, when a stray tabby climbed into her lap. At first demure and coy, she rubbed her head against Chi Chi's thigh. Then with a snooty hiss suddenly sprung round and swiped her left cheek with her wet paw. A scratch of red. The seams of Chi Chi's mouth slanted down as she tried to push it away.

Too late! It sunk its claws deep into the side of her face, ripping open the corner of her left eye. Milky globs of yellow red pus oozed to the bottom of her chin. Chi Chi let out a long piercing scream like a fire whistle.

"Help me! Somebody please!"

Blood slabbered from the cat's mouth, her misshapen teeth chunking down on slivers of flesh.

When it was over, she licked the blood from her whiskers and dropped her tail down as she slunk into the gloom. The skies were clotted with purple clouds, and you could hear the chatter of old men praying over the wind.

THE END

CHIC SAUVAGE

Lullu (Leilah Shazia Arnaz), a shimmery baguette of a woman with ripe Rubenesque hips and lustrous movie star hair that fanned up at the ends like a halo of black daffodils, spent the first fifteen minutes of her day semi-nude swinging over her grand piano. Her eyes half closed with a sanguine look upon her face. As she flew higher and higher a scrim of purply pink light broke through the window.

"Agggh Henry, it's already noon where the hell are you?" Her voice: A posh blend of Sloane Square London infused with a slight ruffle of Paris and a hint of mid-East exotica. When she used her birth language to cuss and curse most people thought she was riffing in Arabic, but it was actually Farsi. Lullu's far flung origins only really manifested themselves when she pronounced certain words. She often put the letters S and K after using nouns and pronouns so darling would become darlingks. It was endearing and stylish in its way. Lullu did her best to explain but most people simply nodded their heads sympathetically and smiled away their ignorance because most people weren't really all that interested. This infuriated her and she would shake her head, click the tip of her tongue and whisper: Tsk tsk until all the bad thoughts inside the turrets of her mind floated away into balloons of fluffy pink clouds.

She'd met Henry on a blind date a few months ago, but all she really knew about him was that he read Politics Philosophy and Economics at Cambridge and worked as a barrister specialising in Environmental law. They'd bonded at an anti-war rally. After chaining themselves to the American Embassy with peace placards, they were arrested and kept their spirits up singing punk anthems in the police van. They both plateaued on the song I'm So Bored With The USA. Of course, they were both acquitted and celebrated their release with Halo burgers and champagne. Ever since then they'd been the almost too perfect perfect couple.

Now she didn't feel the same. Not since she'd spied him on the internet all gussied up in a gold mini-skirt, red wig and stilettos tonguing her ex, Brian. Full on wet kissing. It made her gag. *Bet Brian still stinks of ravioli.* It was one of those intentionally cheesy pics taken at some fundraiser. They were part of a Rocky Horror Tribute skit. *Yuck he tries so hard. Embarrassing. Betrayed me with a pimple butt bigot.* Then she saw more: Coded S&M links, encrypted pics of them in flagrante delicto. And a toxic slurry of vitriol about her and the stream of refugees being let in the country. Brian used to hound her with racial slurs all the time when they argued. *Curry Face, Rag head, Bud bud terrorist* and the piece de resistance *Wacky Paki.* She was almost immune, but she knew the moment *she* had to apologise when *he* mispronounced her name things had to change. *You're too Zrnsitive* he'd say and *so i-zpecial. Deliberately mutilating syllables with that hammy, araby twang.*

She'd clench her teeth and a perverse malignancy would hijack her mind. She wanted to slice his slimy tongue with a carving knife, bite and claw his chest until he drew blood then rip his heart out. She'd thought about using her voodoo kit her grandma bought her. There were spells and feathers inside with magic sand, a miniature rubber doll stuffed with pins and a book of chants. Not bad for twenty squiddleys. Of course, she caved. Instead, she ploughed through two tubs of Ben & Jerry's, Phish food and politely left, sending a courteous note. Now the scum bag was back.

While reading their flirty little exchange, she learned Henry was a wizard at cards and saw a warning shot about his killer allergy. She never even knew Henry had an allergy or that he could literally die from strawberries. She shook her head and clicked the tip of her tongue. Tsk tsk.

As she swung through the air like a punctured swan, she imagined twisting the body of a rat then biting its head off! Higher! Higher! Weeee! She thrust her legs out and landed on the floor with a bounce. After a quick shower she dried off and stepped into a black satin number. Then she fired up her laptop and signed into *Friend Finder. What a fool. Address, dates, everything.* Her mouth was pinched with anger and her hot black eyes ate up the screen with hate.

A couple of hours of mundane office work lulled the time away. Multi-tasking came easy to Lullu. She swallowed a bunch of vitamin pills, a spirulina smoothie and plugged in for ten minutes of auto massage all while typing a work memo. Her thoughts were sporadic covering everything from chicken tikka masala to hairy bikers in pink negligees. She settled on a distorted image of an elderly priest brandishing a chainsaw and concluded everything was an assembly line of FAKERY.

It was a little after three o'clock when Henry finally showed up. His bleached blond hair pomaded to the side and a spotted navy silk square tucked into his jacket pocket. Armed with a huge bouquet of roses and a cutesy little teddy bear. He was the picture of contrition.

"I'm sorry I'm late. Forgive me?"

Lullu's frown broke into a phony smile.

"How can I not?"

They shared a brief kiss and then Lullu turned on the charm.

"Darlingks it's been so long…" And she edged closer to him until her hips grazed his fingers.

As she laid her head against his chest she could tell he wasn't really there, but he tilted his body towards her anyway. He stunk of ravioli. She wanted to splatter the walls with his lies and laurel his affair in gossip print. She couldn't, wouldn't let him DISRESPECT her.

The air was larded with suspicion. Lullu stared straight through the crook of his arm at their newly acquired Cactus plant. Its big meaty leaves looked like the fat swollen fingers of her grandma. She remembered sitting with her every evening after school, watching her spit up blood and milk, warning her about eating the dead and trusting the living. *Grams she used to love ice cream cake reruns of The Golden Girls and anything with Barb -a- r- a -h Stanwyck.* That's how she said it with a rah on the end. Her mind went off again; she felt her face flush when the doorbell chimed.

Instinctively Lullu pulled away. "I'll go." She rushed downstairs and opened the front door.

A courier handed her a flamboyant pink velvet box sealed with a white ribbon. Inside picture perfect strawberries lovingly wrapped in chocolate.

"Package for Ms. Aaaahnaz."

"It's Arnarz."

"Excuse me."

"It's Arn. Never mind."

The courier nodded politely. "Enjoy."

She closed the door and climbed the stairs humming her grandma's favourite English nursery rhyme. "Little Miss Muffet." Her grandma would make her sing along in the kitchen sometimes as she dipped dead spider legs in rose water and stuffed her mouth with crispy fried bat wings. Other traditional delicacies grandma enjoyed included silver fish, flies, red weevils, and mice.

Henry's tone was casual but a little offhand. "Who was it?"

Lullu lowered her eyes until the tips of her lashes caressed her cheek. She hid the box behind her back. "It's a surprise."

Henry nodded her forward.

Lullu drew a short breath and stared at the lines on Henry's face. A morse code of mistakes. She felt her whole body pulse with excitement as she climbed onto his lap and nuzzled his right cheek. It was warm and tufted with sandy stubble.

"Close your eyes. C'mon no peeking."

Reluctantly he agreed.

She plucked a strawberry from the box with her right hand and delicately held it between her thumb and forefinger as her lips brushed his.

Slowly she stroked the back of his neck. "Now open wide."

Henry parted his lips. She jammed the strawberry into his mouth with both hands and stepped back. Within seconds Henry was fitting - writhing - panting – stuttering a slew of incomprehensible death talk. He staggered to the ground clutching his throat. Black glittered blood seemed to pour from his mouth and a dark mushroom glaze veiled his face, as it turned from grey to red then blackish-blue. His tongue had become monstrously large so large in fact it was blocking his airways. His body now lost in a contorted cartoony gargoyleish haze. Lullu left him on the floor with his body shaking violently, while she bustled around quietly humming to herself. With a final jerk of his head, Henry's eyes rolled back into his sockets until they disappeared completely… A strangled scream… And he lay there motionless on the ground.

Lullu stared out of the window at a burst of blinding orange sun then suddenly she saw a big furry spider scuttle across the carpet and crawl over Henry's hand. An ecstatic smile. Her whole face lit up as if it were spangled with hundreds of fairy lights; she closed her fingers on a kiss and watched it suck the blood from Henry's lips.

THE END

UNRESOLVED STORY (Flash)

She's wrapped in biscuit leather and dunked in Lizard high tops. Drunk in the afternoon she stumbles into The Bikini Grill. There's an MTV special on and Debbie's snogging the microphone with her trademark blond shag and her XXS skinny black tee that whispers *X Offender*

A fading bulldog with a big walrus moustache takes a couple of swigs from the bottle and toasts two sequined eyes and a lost dream. He could only think of her silk - lipped smile. It had an exquisite savagery inexcusably GREEDY. A filthy crown of lies atop those gold -red curls.

A crystal waving eco- poet talks in stilted B movie lines.

He wears a rainbow poncho and cut off Levis.

He believes ANARCHY is kool but sews up all the bad ju ju in his life with bum note mantras and sunny talk from new age shiny -shellacked SCAMMERS.

A lemon faced pop prince with rouged cheeks and a nose ring is pissing cherry pink urine in the bathroom stall.

The pimpy DA sealed his mouth with GOLD and together they fell into a dirty secret.
Three stick-up men in black ski masks appear in the doorway and stake their ground. A petite ripple of goodness stares at sunken vampire eyes.

This is the moment where cliché dissolves into a bucket of Terry Gilliam magic.

A flurry of bullets. And a stash of cocaine now that feeling evaporates.

Blood is screaming!

No one wants to talk NOIR theory but there are four dead bodies slumped on cheap plastic seats.

Turn up the Jam! There's two pink ears in the trash can.

A sputtering nightmare.

A gash of regrets in a red satin bra.

An off-duty PI wears his varsity baseball cap back to front and combs the scene looking for MOTIVE.

THE END

RUNNING IN RED X GIRL

Ella B was a butt model, dope dealer, occasional spirit guide and full-time party princess. She ate pimento beans out of a can and lived on throw away caviar and truffles. With her shoulder length whoosh of soft curls and power-popping curves she had that high voltage cultural cachet that made her an instant draw at the biggest, silliest, and often, most scandalous soirees in town. Ella loved to get loose get high do crazy spontaneous things like belly flop naked on bar tops, or dance cheek-to-cheek with strangers at traffic stops. Once she swallowed a ten and a half-inch sword on an empty stomach. Sometimes she'd shout obscene nonsense at ageing celebrities, and at Christmas she'd make mythical, poetic cartoony, paper dolls for homeless grandmas. She always took her clothes off to Billie Holiday and Ray Charles. She said Billie's voice gave her just the right amount of sad and Ray's just the right amount of bad. Her prized possessions included a silver locket with a picture of her dead mother in it and a growing collection of semi-surreal spray paint sketches stacked in the corner of her room. Her favourite: *Suburban-Shopping Mall-Multure Kills*! featured a dying waif in a trailing blooded blanket with a face like Mozart. Ella made art wherever she went floating through the neighbourhood on her own celestial vibe.

I'm riding across Miles Davis's smile. Watching the snake king wash the light from my eyes.

Ella's favourite movie was *Subway*. A glitzy French thriller about a band of poetic misfits who live a carefree existence under the murky tunnels of the Paris Metro. Ella believed she was just like them: lawless an outsider living away from the numbers. She was a throbbing sonata of HOPE except when she heard those fantom voices--sly silk- mouthed violators who slipped their tongues into the cracks of her brain and made her ROAR!

Ella was a stickler for routine despite her airy boho existence. She never left her doll-sized apartment without her signature cat-eyes flicked left to right and was always three vodkas and a slippery nipple away from the ACTION.

At The Palladium a dark smoky but artfully wacky affair, talent was fist-thick, wall-to-ceiling. Ella was all sexed up in silver leather and white thigh highs. A ripple of flashing lights she raised her arms to the booming bass: "Oh baby."

A star child dressed in dreams always looking for something as she feverishly clung onto nothing.

After three booze-bombed hours of THE BIG-TIME guzzling champagne and dancing butt-to-thigh with the star steppers, a goateed lullaby in stretchy gold pants and black hair braided down to his waist slid by. With explosive violet eyes, and a voice thick with the sliding drawl of Texas, he led Ella by the hand and they cha-cha-chaed to WONDERLAND.

Ella stripped down to black lace panties and white sports socks. She read snippets of Sartre in the bathroom as she sucked on juju fruits and filmed herself for a TIK Tok moment she was Tik-toking Satre. Skating across mirrored tiles.

Can you see the black mouth of the skies dropping those satin white butterflies.

A loud urgent knock on the door. Ella was sound asleep, there was no sign of her Texan dream.

A bullish voice knotted with hate chicken-dust and Parisian saxophones. "I know you're in zere!"

Still Ella didn't stir.

"If you don't open up I'll break it down."

A huge hulk of a man, neck as thick as a tree stump and a full grey beard, smashed the door open. He was all trussed up in a pink tutu and red plaid golf shorts cussing in broken English and French.

"Bordel de Merde!"

He scanned the room. His glassy eyes filled with a sick light darting back and forth finally resting on her dinky red purse that lay on the bed stand.

Ella slowly sat up and stared. In the jelly of her mind, she saw HEADLINES: *Man in Ballerina Costume Slays…*

Her mouth widened into a playful little smile. This was obviously a joke. She tossed her head back and laughed and the sound charmed the air like a shim shim shimmer of tambourine kisses.

The man wobbled closer and belched into space. Ella leaned back. His body stunk of warm beer cheap cigarettes and revenge. Yet it seemed oddly familiar to her. His bare chest was ablaze with knife scripted manifestoes written in languages she didn't understand. Ella wondered if he was part of some crazy cult where they wore tutus and had sexy French accents à la Jean Gabin.

A slow dissolve from her hand to the table as she scrambled around for her vape.

The man let out a huge sigh and dropped his face in his hands as he plonked himself down on the edge of a worn red armchair.

"Don't. Don't look at me like that... like I'm a stranger."

Ella was blank and a little woozy. She thought of turning

her phone cam on. A moment of recognition. He looked up at her in-between heavy sobs. The pitch of his voice changed as he shaped his words bending the letters like jazz notes.

"C'est moi. Pierre."

A bearded stutter and then he stumbled into a crazy surrealist pitter patter. "You were a walking talking movie. 90 pounds of red honey I blew the horn and - and we fell steaming - foaming into it. You were a red dream."

His hands moved in a half square to make the shape of an E he mouthed her name ELLA and scripted the air with his fingers.

Faster and faster, he talked. A Charlie Parker beat.

"We were apart from everyone and everything What if what if…"

So many what ifs.

"Merde! Goddam you - the taste of you the smell of you. His hands were flying everywhere. You lived in me until you killed all of me. Now Je ne suis rien. Nothing just shell and bone. Before you - before us pretty plastic-coated smiles the dancing galleria of X girls."

Pierre stole a breath.

Ella scooted to the edge of the bed and grabbed her vape. She stared at the calluses on his right index finger now hardened into a lump and listened to the laugh - hack - wheeze that landed on the carpet. He had aged like a broken melody, but her silent tears had loved him once, loved him enough…to make the stars pop in his mouth.

THE END

THE FUTURE'S A FRAUD

Monday June 7th: Syd began the day with a bump of coke and a scramble of kisses between two sequined strangers. Then he bounced out of bed put a fresh gardenia behind his ear and threw more paint at the canvas. He was completely naked except for a pair of leopard print shorts a big floppy hat and a dizzying look of concentration that ran from the top of his lips to his black forested thighs. An unrepentant man child. He was the ultimate artistic cliché.A caricature of his own hyperbole and insta fame. Syd wanted to say the unsayable with a thousand deft brushstrokes, but he was choking on the blather of goat-cheese nibbling art snobs, and a golden circle of smiling sycophants who worshipped him like a new born deity. His steady stream of male and female lovers were a constant threat to his quiet suited sponsors and a source of irresistible titillation for the tabloids who catalogued his every move. "Am I about to find God?" He screeched and replayed Enya's *Orinoco Flow* on his hi-fi for the seventh time. He whipped off his hat and broke into a clumsy stiff- limbed comedy strut. Lumbering through the air like a potbellied octopus. "Sail away. Sail away sail awayyyyy," he sang, with staccato harshness enunciating each word with poker-faced severity. On the line *We can steer* he squeezed the bulb of his turkey baster and splattered the canvas with a burst of yellow paint.

Syd was trying to scrabble his pieces together for a prestigious gallery opening but something felt wrong. He had one foot stuck in deluded grandeur and the other in the greying cock of the past. All insipid pastels and shrink to fit polyester. He stood up and took a few steps back staring at the drunken splatter on the floor. Syd was petrified that his artsy smartsy scam of peddling pretentious nonsense to the world would finally backfire and secretly convinced his shadow was slowly eating him up from within.

As he pretzeled his ass to the left and right a strawberry-haired fizz bomb in a see-through dress and gladiator boots drifted in: Alice. She had scandal written all over her wonderfully lush thighs. Alice sidled up to him and playfully ran her fingers across his face. In a soft husky alto, she said, "Some people wanna get close to you because they love what you do, and others just want a ringside seat to watch you burn from the inside out."

Celestial Candy

Alice could keep you high for days. She was the kind of person who had no filter and commanded a certain kind of respect strictly reserved for park avenue drug pushers which meant she only catered to the rich the famous and the chosen few.

Feed Your Head

Alice slipped Syd a couple of acid tabs stamped with a cosmic laughing Buddha her calling card. Syd gave her a gentle squeeze on the shoulder and slowly slid one under his tongue. He shimmed on a pair of grey camo pants and was ready for lift off. Alice left a few minutes later when a folly of fashionable, bright things turned up to schmooze and parrrtyyyy. It was a crowd that only Syd could bring together: Traffic stopping hotties, high finance, a sprinkle of well-connected gay hipsters, the odd academic and the ageing avant garde.

T-rippin

The moment the acid hit, Syd shaped his hands around his mouth like a foghorn and bellowed "I am the Messiah. The technicolor Pharoah has arrived!"

A flutter of giggles trailed across the studio as some cute n kissy types edged towards him. He recoiled. His eyes were fixed on a massive red hairy spider that sat regent in one corner of the room feeding on pubic hair and dust. It crawled into his psyche as he listened to a smatter of voices trucking his brain. "Are you screwing her?" He stared at the bristles on his paintbrush. They were moving. Actually moving. *Holy Shit! Those words seemed to be coming from inside the belly of the brush.* Syd's eyes popped: SWOCK! Like two shiny black diamonds as he watched the brush dip flip and twirl through a pot of rusting silver paint. A cone of light curled over a blank canvas and a string of purple dots vibed across his scumbled brushwork. A crazy chain of abstraction floating right before him. First, a talking tear drop, then a dancing green squiggle and all around him an orchestra of confabbing walls. He watched the creamy lush pulp of vicious pigment, plaster the floor with questions. The spider was drowning in a sea of red paint yelling "How could you? You're nothing but a pimp. A stinky pimp."

A sob a scream! Syd ducked "Whoooooo."

And there it was, sailing above the gush of fiery young bodies. A biblical angel straight out of Ezekiel's mouth. Flapping his extra-large feathered wings up and down and belting through the bowels of Syd's sick dystopian canvas as he frenetically spread red over black. Syd rubbed his eyes. "Christ they'll get me. It's only a matter of time…"

The voice had a glistening clarity and burning topaz eyes that glittered from every angle. "You are the tail of Shaitan!"

Was that thing real or irreal? Or was it just Syd gloriously flipping on his trippy - trip acid hit?

Tuesday June 8th 8 a.m. The skies were curdled with grey as they held onto the shadows of the night and dragged a weak limping sun through the haze. Inside the Phoenix gallery Amy Tang sat at her desk in champagne leather and black shades. She was hung over and cranky but with her puff of red curls and Jessica Rabit curves she was still hotter than a Malibu sunrise. The silky-tongued art dealer slash/gallery manager had a cup of Grand Marnier in one hand and a vaping pen in the other. In-between telephone calls she would take a hit then a sip. She leaned back in her chair and put her feet on the table. Always on the scout. Like a well-groomed clarion bird stalking for prey, she worked every angle. Syd was her prize catch, the plat du jour of the art world and Amy had already carved him up into a million little pieces using her client's star power as prime collateral for loans, the purchase of stocks and shares and other illegal legal transactions.

Brrrrr. Brrrr. The classic ring of a landline phone.

Amy's work voice was pinched and prissy. "Yeah this is she. Hmmm. That's right it's called The Liberation of Venus. It's a hundred grand for that piece."

Amy stared nonchalantly at a digital download of two honey dew melons representing female breasts and a piece of blackened Salmon scissored in a V-shape, symbolising the obvious. The whole shebang was hermetically sealed in a plexiglass frame. She flung her legs off the desk and continued the conversation: "No I'm not kidding it's a preservation technique some sort of chemical solution that keeps it fresh. I'll have to check with the artist. I've already had five offers so lemme know by close of play Wed when all bids are off."

Amy was typical of a new breed of art-dealer, she bought works with her ears not her eyes. Yet she was still swimming in colossal debt, despite moonlighting as a private art tutor. Pandering to precocious little park slope pixies pumped on Ritalin every few weeks.

Amy had taken out five different insurance policies with four separate companies just to store, maintain and protect her precious hoardings but she was still forced to pay eye watering premiums for fear of theft. Amy loved discovering the next big thing. The ultimate turn-on but she was never satisfied and had an almost carnal lust for MONEY. She gingerly picked through a stack of bills on her desk and suddenly panic struck. *What if I end up like Linda carting a trash bag of memories across Broadway?*

Just before noon her aunt Judi breezed in cossetted in pink velvet and feathers. Judi, a fifty-five year old failed thespian turned new age "spiritualist" had pale drifting eyes and a kooky vibe, but more importantly she also had a client list that read like a who's who of the rich the very rich and the untouchable.

With a swirl of her hand and a benign smile she asked, "How's my favorite niece?"

"Your only niece."

"What's going on dearie you don't look right."

"So stressed. I've been--"

Judi waggled her finger disapprovingly and made a loud whinnying horse laugh. "Dahling. You're too young and too pretty to be s-t-r-e-s-s-e-d."

Amy tightened her jaw. She hated this part of their relationship.

Judi slid closer and placed both hands on Amy's shoulders.

"Just keep taking your meds and everything will work out peachy."

Amy felt her skin pop. Hives. Little pesky blisters of truth that wended around the back of her neck and across her chest whenever she hit danger mode. She'd been off her meds for weeks.

A trailing scent of coconut and bergamot enveloped the room. Her aunt's signature fragrance: LOVELY. Amy winced. It was anything but and made Amy feel nauseous. She looked around uncomfortably with a bad taste in her mouth. Judi arched her brows into a frown then, rummaged through her purse and pulled out her cheque-book. "How much this time? You know if you keep this up I won't have any rainy day money left. C'mon let's get this over with, so we can have a nice lunch downtown."

And there it was the sarcastic sympathy. Her aunt always had a snide remark to keep her in her place. She gave with one hand and bitched with the other. It made her feel so small.

Amy shook her head. "It's okay. I'll take care of it."

In the manuscript of her life Amy was only days away from bankruptcy and failure. Stashed underneath a ream of papers in her desk drawer was a vicious tax demand from the IRS claiming $20,167 in back taxes, an eviction notice and another heap of bills she hadn't even bothered to look at: credit card statements, gym membership and her monthly subscription to *Art Weekly*. She was about ready to crack under the pressure of it all.

Judi peered at her with a trace of nostalgia. "When your mom was pregnant, I said Cass you're gonna have a girl and she's gonna be trouble well, here we are."

Amy couldn't stand Judi's soft focus reminisce about her mother. It was like the past didn't even exist except for the pretty sanitized version she'd made up. Her mother was a violent drunk hiding behind dime store poetry and soap opera symphonies.

The last memory she had of her was watching her crawl on her belly through the front door on Christmas eve, barefoot in the snow, sporting a black eye a busted lip and a crown made of silver tinsel, and condom wrappers. If it hadn't been for self-righteous Aunt Judi, Amy would have probably ended up at the Children's Home on East 54th Street.

Amy hated Christmas. She glanced at a chattering circle of flies on the windowsill as they licked through the excrement of city sludge and sighed.

"C'mon aunt Judi I gotta a ton of work to do let's get outta here."

They walked three blocks to The Colony Room, a stuffy overpriced restaurant and had veal cutlets and roast potatoes. It always surprised Amy how banal her aunt's palette could be, but she ate everything on her plate and even made room for poached pears with chocolate. Judi looked up, her mouth half-full of pink meat. "I had a meeting with George you know George Lewis, my real estate lawyer. Gave him your number and he promised to buy something, but he said the really big money only starts to roll in when an artist you know crosses over to the other side. When they're six feet under that's when their earning power hits the roof."

Amy leaned forward to listen. The crooked arc of her mind was working overtime. Of course, she knew dead celebrities could generate millions. Marilyn Monroe was synonymous with Chanel No.5, Albert Einstein and Elvis were still making scads of cash and anyone with brand rights to a dead Kennedy was laughing all the way to Wells Fargo and back. Her thoughts became like little poisoned darts as she hypothetically weighed the pros and cons of murder in her mind. *Imagine the tragic death of a young gifted artist…*

A sunny-faced waitress strolled over to their table.

"Can I get you ladies anything else, some tea or our handmade fudge?"

"No thanks, just the check please."

"Alrighty then. When you're ready." She left them a glossy black wallet with an itemized bill inside.

Amy scrolled through each dish and with a nervous smile handed over her credit card.

A couple of minutes later the server returned with a worried look on her face and whispered, "I'm sorry miss your card was declined."

"Oh, that can't be right here try this one."

Judi looked on hesitantly. Amy offered her a reassuring nod.

"It's okay." She mouthed.

Eventually the waitress came back.

"Okie dokie. You're all set."

Judi and Amy linked arms and strolled back to the apartment. Amy pulled out an old photo album and they folded the day away with some lazy chit-chat and peppermint tea. Judi scribbled George's deets down and at around 6 p.m. Amy kissed her aunt on the cheek and waved her goodbye. As she rode the elevator back to the gallery she let a swirl of devilish thoughts nudge her into action.

Despite being listed as one of NYC's premier art dealers Amy secretly loathed art and perversely, only enjoyed looking at mass produced generic shit on eBay. The pictorial equivalent of elevator muzak. She had fallen into her current vocation by lying profusely on all application forms and faking her references. Amy had a way of finagling the truth and wasn't the kind of woman who could deal with failure. She'd rather fake success. That's why she connected so well with Syd they both understood the silky power of IMAGINATION.

Amy's vice: jet-set designer-fuelled luxury. From private club memberships to exquisite diamonds. Every time she bought something EXCLUSIVE it made her feel as if her inner twin were kissed by God. That feeling got into her blood, and she'd laugh and say, "More is More."

It had started out innocently enough, first Amy was late with the bills then she tried deferring them until finally, she stopped paying them altogether. Rent, food, utilities, it had all crept up on her slowly but now she was haemorrhaging cash with no obvious way to stem the flow.

That's when she took out multiple loans using Syd's intel, filled in all the paperwork and bingo! She bought matching designer luggage a fantasy kitchen and the piece de resistance a real Birkin handbag. Amy felt no guilt. She liked to romanticise her actions and didn't think of it as FRAUD or THEFT, to her it was simply a question of "creative accounting." A universal term she liked to fling around that camouflaged the stink of her illegality.

Amy believed artists and agents had a parasitic dependency on one another and felt entitled to exploit Syd by any means necessary. She slung her pocket-book onto the sofa and fired up her laptop. Then she hit the search button:

TOP TEN DRUGS THAT CAN BE FATAL

1. HEROIN
2. COCAINE
3. OXYCODONE

She scrolled through pages and pages of horrifying statistics and gory pictures of the beautiful and the damned. Some had succumbed to suicide, others a fatal combo of drugs and alcohol. Her research confirmed however, that genius shrouded in tragedy was definitely a money spinner and often, a golden ticket to iconic status.

With trembling fingers, she called Cosmo Perry discreet reliable and suitably high-end to supply all the necessaries.

"Come by the Gallery tomorrow night 9.00 pm back entrance."

She felt a hot quiver of excitement as she thought about all the juicy headlines and the endless gravy train of money she could milk, but she remained coldly cynical about her intentions. She ended the call with a zesty sense of achievement and then doomsday terror that morphed into justification. *Syd wants to be immortal… this could be his moment…*

dissolve into pretty star dust and remain the perfect poster boy for America's lost youth. Nobody can resist a dead artist.

It was almost midnight when Amy heard the front door bell ring. She did her best to ignore it, but the ting-a-ling-a-ling of Beethoven's Für Elise continued to seep through the blinds.

"We're closed." She hollered out of the window.

Outside with his fat sweaty hands pressed on the intercom button was TT Murkowski a nasty pimple of a man who also happened to be her landlord. She hurried down to talk to him. He was dressed in black monogrammed velour with shiny white sneakers and an ill-fitting white bucket hat. A sprocket of dandelion fuzz shadowed his cheeks, and his nose was dusted with freckles.

She opened the door just a crack and with an effervescent smile said "Hey TT, great news just done a deal you'll get your money real soon. And, I have an exciting bizzo opportunity if you're interested."

TT shoved his left foot through the door. "I want all the back rent plus next month's money in advance. I don't give a rat's ass who you represent what deal you done or what show you got lined up. If you wanna talk *bizzo* pay up first. I want every penny in my account by 5 p.m. Wed or I'm throwing your sorry ass on the street."

He muttered something about respect and waddled away into the belly of the night with a cheap cigar clenched between his teeth.

Bad Thoughts

Amy was rattled. Her eyes capped with rage. She tried to relax but her mind gave way. She'd have to keep on at TT she knew she could bring him round. She was so tense she kept hearing a chorus of bodiless voices goading her--pushing her to the edge. She remembered the last time it wasn't hard. She'd watched enough crime shows and murder documentaries to deal with the "logistics." The whole bloody episode had lasted less than five minutes. *It all happened in a flash. He tripped-struck his head…* Death was very much part of life as far as Amy could tell and it could happen to anyone anytime anywhere.

Thursday, June 10th Opening Night

Big Val a self-titled "super fabulous anarcho lesbian," was gussied up in pink vinyl. A creature of purring rebellion she was practicing her lines for her big moment in an almost empty room. Just a glass lamp on a scratched table and a rattle of plastic brocade for curtains it was cheap and noisy, but with enough grit to give it some lurid credibility. A downtown celeb for the woman's movement, Big Val was primed for REVOLUTION working on a MANIFESTO OF HONESTY. After she'd read her speech a few times in front of a cracked mirror she sat down and scribbled a note, then she slipped on a black slinky ball gown fishnet stockings and a black latex cat mask. With one last look at the walls she stomped out of the room in bloodied DM boots, packing a 32 caliber ACP in her purse and her VIP ticket to the show.

Once Amy had sweet-talked TT into action vowing to give him two thirds of her inventory she and Cosmo Perry cosied up in her back office. Cosmo a product of blue-blooded dysfunction came from a family worth well over three million, but spent all of his spare time selling drugs and writing gratingly pretentious folk songs. His criminal pursuits having less to do with need and more to do with psychology. So long as he controlled the drug supply Cosmo could party nonstop with a constant stream of hangers on, rich screw-ups and marauding debauchees. He handed over the gear to Amy and they walked three blocks down the street to Syd's showcase. Hard laughter circled the night air, and the evening smog swallowed a nest of secrets.

Friday, June 11th

NEWS FLASH!

> *Tragedy in Brooklyn. We have breaking news just coming in. Three people are dead and five injured after gunfire broke out at Wildies in Water Street.*
>
> *Good evening a star-studded launch party honouring one of the world's most celebrated artists at one of New York's premier art galleries descended into chaos and terror today after a grisly shooting attack.*
>
> *The incident occurred in the early hours of this morning. Eyewitnesses supplied the following footage.*

Amy watched as Syd hopped around on one leg biting his hands screaming. Then bolted upright in her chair and stared hard at the screen, as Syd jumped onto a nearby table pumping his fists in the air as he screeched: "Why be a man when you can be eternal!"

Amy started laughing like a lunatic and couldn't stop. The news anchor lowered her tone and frowned. It hit just the right note.

> *Just a reminder these following images come with a graphic content warning and viewer discretion is advised.*

The 90-second clip showed the gallery temporarily veiled by darkness when a round of six-gun shots was fired. Terrifying screams could be heard across the PA system. The camera then panned around a man sprawled on the floor with his tongue hanging out of the side of his mouth and what appeared to be blood frothing from his lips. Another victim was seen slumped on a chair. The windows were shattered and there was a cryptic message scrawled on the back wall: *The Future's A Fraud.* The footage stopped abruptly, and the anchor switched tone.

> *Police officers say two people died at the scene and a young woman was rushed to hospital with life threatening injuries. Paramedics failed to save her. Investigators are still at the scene and refuse to confirm how many art pieces were stolen, whether the attack was gang related or connected to two, similar incidents in the area. A nationwide hunt has been launched for Syd Du Frais who remains a person of interest...*

An unflattering mugshot of Syd pulled from CCTV footage was displayed across the screen. TT called Amy from his apartment, he had a gallery's worth of stolen art inside.

"Let's close this deal."

In Fat Lola's a greasy little dive on the sly end of Chelsea everything was on offer. Syd's eyes bulged at the TV report as a vampy brunette in crushed velvet sidled up to him.

"It was that bitch agent of mine. She caused this. She had all my information. Social security number bank details everything. I mean the shots came outta nowhere it was dark oh man that was close. Bitch wiped me out even stole my name with an NFT. Know what an NFT is?"

The woman stared at him blankly.

"A cat meme for six mill."

A bitter smile, Syd laughed at the jokes inside his head and continued his one-note monologue until the woman drifted away. If she knew who he was she didn't care. He looked around. No one was even watching the TV their noses were buried in their phones, so he sat there undisturbed knocking back the Courvoisier and hallucinating…

A strong sense of déjà vu. Syd was about to leave when Amy trundled in flanked by two of TT's snarling heavies: Quack Quack and Whack Whack. Syd saw a winged lion and two sphinxes in the neon strip of his mind.

Dirty Lickins

Amy was brandishing an empty glass jar. Inside a price tag of $10,000. Syd made a grab for it and shrieked "Those are my thoughts in there my thoughts."

The two goons dragged Syd kicking and screaming into the back room. They pushed him onto a chair and strapped him down with duct tape.

Amy managed a big smile. "Don't look at me like that Syd. There's no empathy here. So cheap." She huffed. "You want empathy? Wanna feel better? Find a therapist or suck up a bunch load of Prozac."

Her mouth had become a vicious red line. "Don't worry it's not gonna be that bad and when we're done you'll be even more of a global sensation. Trust me."

She nodded at the help. THWONK! BLAT! A beer bottle bounced off the side of Syd's head.

Syd toppled over with glass in his eyes and Amy let the grade Z movie-mob-squad maul and malign with impunity. Whack Whack murmured "Let's Go." And careened towards Syd with the butt of his 38c revolver.

A splatter fest of blood pulp and near DEATH.

Amy looked repulsed. "Who the fuck am I?"

Three months later:

"Good evening ladies & gentleman and welcome to Sotheby's New York for this historic sale. Tonight, we give you: *Elegy to the Painter's Arm*, featuring the severed arm of SYD Du Frais, Artist Provocateur and self-styled gonzo art king making a gloriously irreverent spectacle of gore with his very own arm, perfectly preserved in formaldehyde enhanced with real gold fingers."

A record-breaking bid. Amy raked in over a million dollars and had a tax burning party. She phoned George. "You were right! The arms of greatness can give you wings!"

She bounced around undisturbed in her own petal of light schmoozing with the rich the dirty and the dangerous.

Just then, Big Val marched over clutching a pink slip of paper.

She tapped Amy politely on the shoulder. "Ms Tang."

No response. Just the briefest of glances and a steely look of arrogance.

Big Val tapped her on the shoulder again and with a deep breath huffed: "Ms. Tang you've been ghosting me for months. I've left dozens of messages. You never even bothered to reply. Like I wasn't worth three fucking lines of your time. All I got was THIS sent to me over a year ago."

She waved the document in Amy's face like a loaded gun. A sales receipt for a bolshy AGITPROP work she'd spent months crafting.

Amy remembered it now. *An ugly piece of subliterate junk* that's what the culture critic from *Art Roxx* had claimed yet she'd still managed to palm it off on some reality TV star, for oodles of cash. But Amy hadn't paid Big Val a penny for her work; not one lousy dime.

She shooed her away with a fake smile and the standard brush -off. "I don't recall, I'll just get Poppy my assistant." Then she disappeared into a VIP-cushioned bubble and left Big Val hanging.

A trigger point response. Big Val was fuming. *So tired of being invisible.*

She scurried after her and cornered Amy on the stairway. In a low raspy voice, she said: "I'm not like you Ms Tang. I can't cheat decent honest people out of what's theirs. TRUTH triumphs over everything. I know you sold my piece, I saw it on TV hanging on some celebrity's wall."

Big Val had an angry cast to her mouth and her spunky

embattled eyes blew hot. "You STOLE from me. I'm living on stale promises and dime-sized bags of Cheetos." She paused and looked around.

"While you've got all this."

A bemused stare. "I'm sorry what's your name? Anyway, doesn't matter, I thought my…"

Big Val pulled out her gun from her purse and fired. But nothing happened because the safety catch was on. Amy let out a sadistic little laugh as she searched for her security team. No one was in earshot.

Phat flashy bursts of orange and blue neon spelled out the word F-R-A-U-D on the main wall when Big Val finally released the safety, but she couldn't pull the trigger. She dropped the gun on the floor and fled, bumping into Syd on her way out. He reached for the gun with his good hand then with a vengeful little smile took aim:

Pop! Pop! Pop!

Amy's face paled and she fell to the ground as the bullet smashed through the air and struck the left side of her head, finally lodging itself in the back of her skull. A dissonant flame of screams pierced the room. The language of blood was everywhere: Gushing spurting spraying draining. Syd stooped down and whispered: "The One-Armed Death Chancer it's my finest work."

Police and paramedics crashed the scene as the night stuttered into dawn with a plague of lost souls ghosting the sidewalk.

THE END

About the author

Saira Viola is a pioneering novelist and poet. Her experimental sonic scatterscript style has been critically acclaimed by literary heavyweights Benjamin Zephaniah and Heathcote Williams.

"She creates a star sourced punkish take on the human condition and her work is whirlwind of larks and linguistics and the dark and light in between."

Also by Saira Viola

- *Jukebox*
- *Crack, Apple & Pop*

More books from Fahrenheit Press

The Beloved Children

Three young women; Chrysanthemum, Rose & Orage are thrown together performing as The Three Graces on the stage of Fankes' Theatre during the closing days of the Second World War.

It's there they come under the spell of wardrobe mistresses Dolores and Janna – a chance encounter that will guide and change all of their fates forever.

Set in the dying days of vaudeville theatre and laced with mysticism, fortune tellers, ghosts, and evocative descriptions of the closing days of the War – The Beloved Children will literally make you laugh out loud and perhaps even shed the odd tear.

The Beloved Children is wise, funny, heart–breaking, joyous, poignant, and entirely entirely enthralling.

Tina Jackson has conjured characters that you will fall unapologetically in love with and placed them in a world that you won't want to leave.

This book genuinely weaves a spell around the reader and once you make friends with Janna, Dolores, and The Three Graces you'll never want to be without them in your life again.

"This gloriously offbeat tale has shades of Angela Carter, with its beguiling characters weaving a magical spell." – Kitty Marlow, The Mail On Sunday

Pure by Jo Perry

Caught in a pincer movement between the sudden death of Evelyn (her favourite aunt) and the Corona virus, Ascher Lieb finds herself unexpectedly locked down in her aunt's retirement community with only Evelyn's grief–stricken dog Freddie for company.

As the world tumbles down into a pandemic shaped rabbit–hole Ascher is wracked with guilt that her aunt was buried without the Jewish burial rights of purification.

In order to atone for this dereliction of familial duty, Ascher – in her own words 'a profane, unobservant, atheist Jew, frequent liar and grieving loser' –volunteers to become the newest member of Valley Haverim Chevra Kadisha, a Jewish burial society on–call twenty–four–seven during lockdown and performing Mitzvot at no cost to the bereaved.

What follows is a journey through the insanity of lockdown in Los Angeles as Ascher attempts to bring peace to a troubled soul, and perhaps in the end redemption for herself.

This novel is everything.

In the hands of a lesser–writer a novel set in the time of covid could lead to a cliché ridden trope–fest, but instead with the skill and grace we've come to expect from Jo Perry she has delivered a book that is wise and beautiful and uplifting.

In our opinion with *Pure*, Jo Perry has surpassed even her own high–bar and written the finest novel of her career to date – but don't take our word for it – here's what some of her fellow writers say…

"Faultlessly imagined and beautifully written, this is one of the best novels I've read all year." –Timothy Hallinan, author of the acclaimed Simeon Grist series

<u>The Perception of Dolls by Anthony Croix</u>

"It's almost as if history is trying to erase the whole affair." – Anthony Croix

The triple murder and failed suicide that took place at 37 Fantoccini Street in 2001, raised little media interest at the time. In a week heavy with global news, a 'domestic tragedy' warranted few column inches. The case was open and shut, the inquest was brief and the 'Doll Murders' – little more than a footnote in the ledgers of Britain's true crime enthusiasts – were largely forgotten.

Nevertheless, investigations were made, police files generated, testimonies recorded, and conclusions reached. The reports are there, a matter of public record, for those with a mind to look.

The details of what took place in Fantoccini Street in the years that followed are less accessible. The people involved in the field trips to number 37 are often unwilling, or unable, to talk about what they witnessed. The hours of audio recordings, video tapes, written accounts, photographs, drawings, and even online postings are elusive, almost furtive.

In fact, were it not for a chance encounter between the late Anthony Croix and an obsessive collector of Gothic dolls, the Fantoccini Street Reports might well have been lost forever.

Cash Rules Everything Around Me by Rob Gittins

Morrissey Jarrett is fresh out of prison and back on the streets of his hometown Cardiff.

During his enforced absence the city has been re–developed to within an inch of its life and a disoriented Morrissey falls back into old habits as he scams, schemes, and steals whatever he needs to survive.

Morrissey has big dreams though. Dreams of making one last huge score, dreams of leaving his life of crime behind, dreams of reuniting with the love of his life and dreams of walking off into the sunset with her. Happy. Ever. After.

All he needs is a plan.

Luckily, the circles Morrissey frequents provide ample opportunities for ill–gotten gains and soon the perfect job literally falls into his hands.

And so, along with a hastily assembled crew of misfits, Morrissey embarks on planning the perfect heist. With all their eyes fixed steadily on a payday that could change their stars forever – all they have to do is keep their heads down, play it cool, and follow the plan to the letter.

What could possibly go wrong?

Black Moss by David Nolan

In April 1990, as rioters took over Strangeways prison in Manchester, someone killed a little boy at Black Moss.

And no one cared.

No one except Danny Johnston, an inexperienced radio reporter trying to make a name for himself.

More than a quarter of a century later, Danny returns to his home city to revisit the murder that's always haunted him.

If Danny can find out what really happened to the boy, maybe he can cure the emptiness he's felt inside since he too was a child.

But finding out the truth might just be the worst idea Danny Johnston has ever had.

"As one would expect from a writer with the skill and experience of David Nolan, this haunting book deals with very difficult issues in an incredibly sympathetic manner while at the same time throwing a light onto one of the most complicated and shaming areas of our society – the failure to protect those who are the most vulnerable."

To read more of the best, most inspiring fiction in the world visit us at our website.

www.Fahrenheit–Press.com

www.ingramcontent.com/pod-product-compliance
Lightning Source LLC
Chambersburg PA
CBHW020332310726
48979CB00015B/2338/J

* 9 7 8 1 9 1 4 4 7 5 7 3 3 *